ALMOST

ALSO BY ROSIE ROWELL

Leopold Blue

ALMOST GRACE

ROSIE ROWELL

HOT
KEY
BOOKS

First published in Great Britain in 2015 by Hot Key Books
Northburgh House, 10 Northburgh Street, London EC1V 0AT

A CIP catalogue record for this book is available from the British Library.

ISBN: 978-1-4714-0127-5

1

This book is typeset in 10.5 Berling LT Std using Atomik ePublisher

Printed and bound by Clays Ltd, St Ives Plc

www.hotkeybooks.com

Hot Key Books is part of the Bonnier Publishing Group
www.bonnierpublishing.com

You are a child of the universe, no less than the
trees and the stars;
you have a right to be here.
And whether or not it is clear to you, no doubt
the universe is unfolding as it should.

Max Ehrmann, *Desiderata*

FRIDAY

At this time of day it is important to have something to do. It doesn't matter what – the secret is in the doing. Holes in the day leave too much space for hungry thoughts to come creeping out. But as I'm currently wedged into the back corner of Brett's new car, next to a pile of duvets and pillows with my feet resting on three crates of beer, doing anything other than breathing is proving a challenge. This triggers one of Mum's fridge-decorating mantras: '*Breath is life. When we channel our breath, we transform our lives.*' The words are written around a candle flame against a black background. The smug, flowery script makes you want to transform yourself into a drop-out crackhead. I shift around and channel my breath onto the window I've been leaning against, employing a Darth Vader noise, until it is so fogged up that the car next to us is nothing more than a smudge.

Because the air con does not quite reach my corner this takes a fair bit of time. But we have plenty of that. We have not moved for the past ten minutes.

I frown at the glass, not sure what to draw. What would Louisa draw? What would be clever, ironic and amusing at the same time? Only I could turn car-window graffiti into an existential crisis.

The car ahead of us erupts into sound, as if it's releasing gas.

'Who are you even hooting at?' sighs Brett from the driver's seat.

'He is hooting at his life,' I reply, still staring at my window. I try for a retro campervan and write *roadtrip!!* next to it, but it looks like a childish school bus, so I wipe that away and start again. This time I go for curly wave patterns, which are even more child-like but at least they're not trying to be anything else.

'This traffic is nothing compared to Jozi,' says Louisa in the passenger seat. She's been making a holiday playlist. Her taste in music is eclectic to say the least.

Brett catches my eye in the rearview mirror. 'In *Joburg* traffic jams last three days.'

I laugh. 'In Jozi a man died in a traffic jam. No one knew until the queue started moving a week later.'

'But at least in Jozi rush hour doesn't start at two o'clock on a Friday,' counters Louisa.

'You can take a girl out of the mine dumps . . .' says Brett, winking at me.

Louisa tuts. 'You people with your little mountain and your freezing sea . . .' she replies in a withering voice. She and her family moved to Cape Town more than four years ago but Louisa still breathes Joburg air. She is a child of the city. Her reactions to even mild exposure to nature provide Brett and me with endless material to tease her.

2

A movement in the car next to us catches my attention. The driver is waving at me. For a moment I'm confused. Then I realise he's interpreted my car art as trying to get his attention. I burst into high-pitched laughter and turn away.

'What?' Louisa turns around again.

'The guy in the car next to us thinks I've been waving at him,' I say, feeling myself grow hot.

'Nice work, Grace – he's probably some kind of pervert who is going to follow us all the way up to Baboon Point.'

At last we start to move. The cars that have been stacked around us seem to miraculously disappear and the road opens up. Louisa turns back to me. 'Did your mum sit you down for the serious chat this morning about men with evil intent?'

I smile. 'No. She'd gone to work by the time I got up.'

'Lucky you,' Louisa says and rolls her eyes.

'Did your mum say anything about the evil intent of eighteen-year-old boys?' Brett inclines his head towards Louisa.

Louisa laughs in her deep, gravelly way and ruffles his blonde hair. 'Luckily for you, she didn't.'

I turn and look out of the window. *You're wrong, Lou. That's exactly what Brett wants.* He wants Mrs Cele, Louisa's mother, to refer to him as Louisa's boyfriend, not 'that little friend who makes me laugh'. And I would have given anything for Mum's 'chat' last night to have been about boys.

With the Mother City and the mountain behind us, the scenery settles down into wide-open scrubland with a slash of blue Atlantic on our left. If we kept driving north, little

3

would change before we reached Namibia and eventually the Skeleton Coast.

'When do we get to Hermanus?' asks Louisa. Hermanus is a pretty seaside town on the East Coast, famous for being the breeding ground of Southern Right whales. Some of Mum's weirder yogi friends spend weekends there during breeding season 'calling' to the whales.

Brett laughs. 'Wrong coast.'

'What?'

'The ocean on your left is the Atlantic.' Brett catches my eye again. 'You do know that South Africa has two coastlines, right?'

Louisa smacks his arm and turns to look out of the window.

I feel a stab of guilt. When Helen suggested Baboon Point as an alternative to the mess of school-leavers getting out of control at the 'Plett Rage', I knew that Louisa didn't know what she was agreeing to. In these couple of weeks post exams, eighteen-year-olds from across the country descend on Plettenberg Bay to gorge on their new-found freedom. We've chosen a different option, but Louisa is still expecting lush and pretty seaside villages, not the wind-blasted, craggy coastline we're headed for. Initially, it was a childish twist of jealousy that kept me quiet. Then I realised that Baboon Point is my idea of paradise: the beach is at least ten kilometres long and the town is so small and remote that the chance of being caught up in a week of wild parties is negligible.

'Brett! What the fuck is that?' Louisa tugs on his arm. 'What *is* that?'

'Koeberg Nuclear Power Station.'

'We are going on holiday next to a nuclear power station?'

This is why I love Louisa – she announced we were going to Baboon Point and now it's Brett's fault.

'No, we're going much further up the coast.' He looks at her. 'But you should see the weird fish you get in this bay.'

Louisa looks at him then slumps in her seat. There is a rumble of words from her that even if I could speak Zulu I wouldn't understand.

'Ntombifuthi, leave the ancestors alone,' says Brett in Mrs Cele's voice, grinning at me in the rearview mirror. He has no idea what she's saying either. We learnt Xhosa at junior school, and not very successfully. Louisa's Zulu name, which means 'it's another girl' irritates her intensely. Her mother uses it often, and pointedly, when Louisa's being stubborn.

'You liked the online picture of the house, Lou,' I say.

'Yes, Grace, I liked the *house*. No one mentioned that we are on a nuclear-active coastline. We'll come back with radiation poisoning.'

'And two heads,' says Brett.

Louisa turns off her playlist. 'What are we going to do here for a week?' she demands.

'The surfing is great,' says Brett.

Louisa dismisses it with a click of her tongue.

'It has sunsets,' I offer.

'Sunsets! Everywhere has sunsets, Grace.'

Louisa reaches for a tray of mini cupcakes. Brett tries to help himself but she smacks his hand away. 'Why didn't you tell me about this?'

Brett laughs. 'You arranged it with Helen. I thought you knew.'

'Does Helen know?'

'Of course. Everyone knows the West Coast.'

She makes a face at him, then turns and passes the tray back to me. Suddenly her face lights up. She winks and flashes a knowing smile.

'That's not even funny,' I say, taking the tray.

'Don't fight it, Gracie.'

In our final school magazine, the 'matric tribute' edition, there was a section devoted to 'Most Likely To . . .' I was lying in the sun at lunch break, with my head on Louisa's leg, reading it aloud. Louisa was most likely to become the first female president. Although she dismissed it, I knew she was secretly pleased. I was most likely to run a cupcake company.

'A cupcake company? Where does that come from?'

'You know, like the cute girl in *Bridesmaids*,' said Louisa, laughing. It's easy to laugh when you're the president.

'The fucked-up one with the *failed* cupcake company.'

'You can do all the cupcakes for my state occasions.' Louisa patted the top of my head. 'What does it predict for Brett?'

'Mechanic. That's worse, right?'

When Louisa has turned back in her seat, my cupcake joins the handful of NikNaks and bunch of grapes in the sandwich bag in my pocket. I think back to Mum last night, home from her hot yoga, staring at me as if I was insane. I was yelling at her, I couldn't help it. '*Rory said a lot of things, all of which are bullshit!*' It strikes me that what is particularly tragic about that conversation, particularly representative of my life, is that while Louisa's mother was preaching to her about unwanted male stranger-danger, I was yelling at my mother about a middle-aged man who had effectively 'dumped' me six weeks ago and yet is still messing up my life.

'Helen's texted to say there's a house party on tonight,' says Louisa.

'Awesome,' I reply with a thud in my stomach.

She turns around. 'You sure?' she says with those watchful eyes.

'Of course!'

A year ago, I would have meant it. I would have been planning what to wear and demanding to know who else would be there. But over the past few months I've developed a habit of crying at parties – it has something to do with watching everybody else looking effortlessly happy. It makes things awkward, so I do my best to avoid them. The very low point was the school leavers' dance – I didn't even get there. I saw Mum's expression in the mirror when I put my dress on – a mixture of heartbreak and horror – and went into the bathroom and made myself sick so that I didn't have to go. Apparently my partner – a friend of a friend – got so drunk at the 'before' party that he was sent home.

By the time we stop at the Shell Ultra City my bladder is about to rupture from the need to pee. The air outside is different to Cape Town. It's hotter and drier. The sky seems bigger with each kilometre that we travel. A week away from my head and my life and my mother's double negatives: 'We are not not going to talk about this, Grace.' I do a cartwheel next to the car to make Louisa laugh.

Safely inside the loo cubicle I open the sanitary bin and deposit the bag of snacks.

'Grace!' Louisa's voice is just the other side of the divide and makes me jump.

'What?'

'Don't sit on the seat!' she says and giggles.

'You're just like my mother,' I say.

'Do you have loo paper?'

I pass a wad of it to her under the cubicle wall.

'We should have gone to Plett,' Louisa says as we're washing our hands.

'Nah, you're going to love it,' I reply. 'I promise.' I look at the two of us in the mirror. A few days ago I cut my hair short and bleached it. It looked good at the hairdresser's. Mum's only comment was 'Is this a Miley Cyrus thing?'.

'No, it's an Agyness Deyn thing,' Louisa replied for me.

'Is that better?' asked Mum, looking back at my hair with those permanent frown lines.

Louisa keeps her hair cropped close to her skull. It drives her mother crazy. 'It's so ugly. Why do you want to look like a boy?'

'Why do you want to walk around with fake hair?' is Louisa's reply.

She looks up now and catches my eye and starts belting out the lyrics to 'Ebony and Ivory' into an imaginary mike.

I join in, harmonising, just as we'd spent hours practising – and we both start laughing.

Louisa and I have been friends since the first day she arrived at school. We used to be a girl band. We called ourselves Lace. 'Half part Grace, whole part soul.' We rehearsed at Louisa's house to begin with, until her sister paid us a monthly rate not to practise there. After that we set up our studio in the spare room at mine. At first we recorded CDs of our favourite covers, and made countless tribute videos. Our signature look was each of us wearing an elbow-length lace glove. I'd found the pair at the back of my mum's cupboard. We thought the nod to Jacko showed how sophisticated we were.

Then we decided Lace needed to move in a new direction and started writing our own songs, one or two ballads, but mostly rap.

Some days we all are prone
To feel that we're alone
No one calling on the phone
But if you stop and stare
There are people everywhere
Who need someone to care
We might get in your face,
But that's who we are, we're Lace.

We thought we were achingly cool. It was only a matter of time before we'd win *The X Factor* and tour the country.

Brett auditioned for an Eminem-type role – his looks are perfect – but he didn't pull it off. He was our beatbox and our groupie. Truthfully, he would have dressed up like a donkey just to be able to hang out with Louisa.

For about four months we wrote a blog, 'Keeping Pace with Lace', and recorded a live interview with 'DJ Brett' when our single 'Prone' reached number one. It actually got two hundred hits on YouTube (and a lot of abuse). Then one day it just seemed silly. It's like that cringey feeling when you read old diary entries – you know you wrote the words but the feelings don't belong to you any more. These days I get that cringey feeling pretty much every time I speak.

I look at Louisa. 'What was the official line about why Lace split up?'

Louisa shakes her head sadly. 'Usual story: "financial problems".'

We share a smile in the mirror. The moment is broken by my stomach starting to rumble.

'Are you still hungry?' asks Louisa.

I shake my head. 'Indigestion.'

Louisa gives me a look but leaves it at that. I follow her back to the car. She and Brett make a far better ebony and ivory. They make each other seem more exotic. Louisa makes Brett's side-sweep of surfer hair and blue eyes look authentic; Brett makes Louisa look like a regal African queen. Could anyone balance me in that way? I resemble an anaemic, odd-looking boy – who in the world would complement that?

Brett is right – Baboon Point is much further up the coast than the nuclear power station. We pass turn-offs for well-known beach resorts and, later, turn-offs for nature reserves. It feels as if we've run out of turn-offs and we're going to keep following the coastline north through seemingly endless scrub bush and distant hills that look more like air bubbles under the earth's surface. I must have nodded off, because I jerk as Louisa shouts, 'Baboon Point!' and claps her hands.

As we follow the signs into town we pass a sprawling township with a large soccer stadium in the middle of it.

At first glance Baboon Point could be a ghost town, or after-hours on a movie set. Brett parks outside a downbeat cafe. As we get out and stretch, the change in the air in startling. It is hot and dry and salt-heavy all at the same time. After the crush of Cape Town's mid-afternoon traffic, the emptiness and space feels unbalancing. The shop seems deserted until my eyes adjust to the gloom and I make out the cashier in the corner behind an electric fan. The shelves are stocked with fizzy drinks, instant coffee, matches, toothpaste and loo paper – the kind of things you leave at home on a weekend away. It has a 'deli' counter, with some thirsty-looking samoosas and a large roll of lurid pink polony. *Mmm, ground-up pigs' trotters mixed with pink slime.* When I asked the shopkeeper if she has any celery, she frowns at me and says, 'We don't stock herbs.'

There are two cars parked outside the police station and one outside the hotel opposite. By the time we find the estate agent's house to pick up the key for our house, it's late afternoon. There is a hot wind blowing. The woman looks at us dubiously. Her hair is a deep maroon-red. She's wearing an orange tracksuit that emphasises her vast stomach.

'Please remember to lock the outside rubbish bins as the baboons make a disgusting mess,' she says as she examines the cheque my mum sent up as a deposit for breakages.

'Real, live baboons?' Louisa asks.

The woman nods. 'And keep your house locked when you're out or they will move in before you're back.'

'Perfect,' mutters Louisa. 'Any other forms of wildlife we should expect?'

'Well, of course the *boomslangs*<?> Venomous tree snake, but we haven't had any reports of them on your property,' the lady replies in an uninterested tone. I can't tell whether she's simply trying to get a rise out of Louisa, but it's working.

'Where are the shops?' asks Louisa.

This makes the lady laugh. 'I hope you didn't come here to shop. You passed the cafe on the corner; that one with the big Coke sign. Then there's the Chinese one over the road.'

'Is that it?' asks Louisa.

'No, there are the two liquor stores,' replies the woman as she pushes a piece of paper for us to sign. 'And the hotel and the *Kreef Kombuis*<?> Crayfish Kitchen restaurant, but that's not open this week, and the *Strandloper*<?> Beachcomber bar. I wouldn't go there if I were you. Oh – and the police station.' She ends with emphasis. 'For anything else, you need to go to Lambert's Bay. Enjoy your stay. I hope I do not hear from you.'

As we turn to go, a sound like distant thunder makes us stop. It grows louder, as though it's coming straight for us. 'What in God's name is that?' says Louisa.

'Ag, it's the train,' the lady says with a flick of her hand. 'Transporting iron ore down to Saldahna,' she adds at the sight of our blank faces. The noise continues, unrelenting.

'How do you stand it?' says Louisa.

'I don't even hear it any more,' says the woman and she closes her front door.

Eventually the noise fades away into the afternoon. 'Well, this is super,' mutters Louisa. 'I wonder if my mother knew about the train.'

We get a closer look at the track as we follow the directions to our house. It's like a rusty slash running across the land. Louisa's mouth is in a tight line. 'Helen didn't mention any of this,' she mutters.

12

Our house looks promising from the road. It is the last one in a row along the seafront; a white clapboard cottage perched on stilts. The entrance to the drive is partly hidden by the coastal bush that borders the house. The bottom of Brett's car scrapes on something hard as we park under a Brazilian Pepper tree. Mum had a Brazilian Pepper removed from our garden because it was an 'aggressive alien species'. Unfortunately it was also a very good windshield and the garden has never quite recovered.

'Oops,' says Louisa, 'was that a stone?'

Brett gets out. 'Nope, a root.'

The house is perfect. As we get out the car I feel a child-like excitement about this week for the first time. The pictures on the booking site were nice but seeing it in front of us makes our week away suddenly real. Steps lead up to a large wooden deck that overlooks the long, white, gleaming beach. A dream beach for running. I walk to the edge of the deck and lean against the railing. To the left the bay ends where a hill meets the sea in a rocky point. Up against the rocks on the shoreline is a set of long low buildings. 'What are those?' I point.

'Crayfish factory,' replies Brett. Even though they're at the other end of the bay, the buildings have a forlorn look about them.

In the other direction it looks as though the beach could carry on all the way up to Namibia.

'Magic,' smiles Brett, standing next to me.

'Yay!' I say and give him a hug.

There is a big wooden table and chairs on the deck. 'Perfect for sundowners,' I comment.

'Fuck sundowners,' says Brett, and flips the lid off a

13

bottle of beer. His luggage consists primarily of beer and his surfboard.

Louisa appears on the other side of Brett. It's hard to remember that Brett and I were friends before Louisa arrived. We've been friends since we started school; the two smallest kids in the class.

'See, Lou – we've got our own private path down to the beach.' I point to a winding trail that cuts through hip-height bushes to the sand. 'And that's a serious beach.'

'Ja, ja, and let me guess – the water is as warm as a bath.'

Brett and I look at each other and laugh. 'Nope!'

Inside, the house seems to be suffering an identity crisis. The long dumpy sofa and mismatched armchairs look as though they've come straight out of someone's granny's sitting room. There is a heavy round dining table and a large bookshelf stuffed with paperbacks and board games. But the rest of the living area is white – the walls, the ceiling, the floor. Sunshine pours in through the wide windows on either side of the room. Louisa comes and stands next to me. She nods her head approvingly. 'Beach chic,' she announces.

I smile at her. 'A whole week without parents!' This week away has been a marker in our minds for years – our rite of passage from childhood into adulthood – and it has finally arrived. In a rush I reach out and hug her. I feel her return the hug but then stiffen slightly and pull back. I've come to recognise that reaction – Mum's friends do it all the time. It's normally followed by, "*You've lost so much weight!*" 'Let's see the rest of the house,' I say quickly and turn away to avoid her eye.

There is a small kitchen, a bathroom and two bedrooms. 'I know, I know,' I say loudly, choosing the smaller room with two single beds. 'Please keep the bonking down.' I dump my bag on the near bed and look around. The floor is covered in sisal matting; on the wall are three sepia prints in driftwood frames. My phone rings – it's Mum. I flick it to silent. From Louisa and Brett's room comes the sound of laughing; the click of the door closing quietly. I sit down on the bed. Whatever. It's not their fault they're happy. This week I will run and chill and figure out a way to get around Mum.

The end of the day glimmers faintly on the horizon as we walk along empty roads, following Helen's directions to the house holding the party. 'It would be pretty creepy to live here all year around,' I say, looking at the few lit-up houses amongst their darkened neighbours.

'Just you and the baboons,' says Louisa. But there is also a feeling about this deserted town that tugs at me. You must feel a certain wildness and energy living beside this untamed coast. I know Louisa would think me deranged if I tried to explain this, though, so I keep it to myself.

The party house appears to have no roof. Music and light and voices spill out over high terracotta walls. Louisa speeds up as we approach. I know that feeling. We used to sneak out all the time from her house on a Saturday night. Her father snores so loudly you could land a helicopter in their garden and no one would notice. Tonight I feel my feet growing heavy.

We make our way through the maze of parked cars and enter

the house through the open door on the side. As soon as we step inside, the house makes sense. It's built like a Moroccan fortress, with a kitchen and living area opening into a large courtyard. There is a break in the music. The clumps of bodies all seem to stop talking and look around, making our arrival more obvious. Then one of those summer dance anthems starts playing and they turn away again, like a weird game of musical statues. Louisa looks back and winks at me.

'Louisa!' calls Helen's voice. It seems to be coming from the group standing near a tree in the courtyard. Fairy lights twinkle from its branches. Louisa's smile grows wide. She waves and makes her way towards the group. I turn away and bump straight into Theresa.

She is unnecessarily pretty, with big brown eyes and soft shiny hair to match. She's had boyfriends since pre-school. Our mums are best friends. They met in the maternity ward; Theresa is two days older than me. 'Ooh, twins!' everybody used to say. I don't remember her dad – her parents got divorced a long time ago, so we were dumped together at every social event. 'Isn't it nice they have each other!' our mums' friends would say, meaning *Thank God they don't have to hang around us all afternoon.* Theresa had a way of behaving like an angel in front of the grown-ups, but when we were sent off to play, she made it clear that we weren't friends. It doesn't bother me any more.

Tonight she's wearing a blue dress with skimpy straps to show off her beautiful collarbones.

'Wow! Your hair!' she says, tilting her head to the side. It takes me a moment to remember my chopped-off, peroxided new look. In a glance she manages to destroy the hairdresser's pronouncement of 'ultra funky' and makes me feel like an attention-seeking child. 'It's so . . . *you*!' she laughs and pulls a hand through her glossy mane.

'Isn't it?' I nod, adopting her fake voice. But annoyingly she doesn't get the sarcasm.

'How are you?' She tries to take my hand, her Bambi eyes large.

'Fine.' Until a few months ago, 'LouandGrace' used to be said as one word at school. But increasingly Louisa has been hanging out with Helen and Theresa. I know that everyone has noticed the shift and no doubt has been talking about it. I can see it in Theresa's eyes.

'My mum said you're going to an eating disorder clinic.' Theresa speaks in a hushed voice reserved for the sick and dying.

'I'm not. I'm going to university, just like you.'

'Oh, OK,' she says in an annoyingly disbelieving way.

I don't want to hear any more of what she might have to say. 'I'm going to get a drink,' I say abruptly and walk away.

I can't see Lou or Brett but it seems as though while I was talking to Theresa about fifty people have walked into the house; it's packed. As I walk off, I know that if I look back, Theresa will be talking to one of the other girls, looking in my direction, so I step out into the courtyard. There must be people here I know, but the thought of finding them and thinking up something to say makes me feel very tired. In the far corner of the yard is a glowing fire pit. I don't recognise anyone gathered around it and sit down gratefully on the edge of the group. It's moments like this that I think seriously about

17

taking up smoking. Maybe I should just carry a pack around so that I can light one up and look as though I have a reason for being on my own.

I can pick out Louisa's laugh above the noise. Mum says you can always hear the sound of your own child crying above all the others; it's that way with Louisa's laugh. The first thing teachers did at the beginning of each year would be to seat Louisa and me at opposite ends of the classroom. 'We've heard about you two,' they'd say, nodding. But we didn't need to be sitting near each other. A look across the classroom was enough to set us off.

There is a nudge in my ribs. A hand next to me is holding a bottle of tequila. I look up. More people have joined the group around the fire since I sat down. The guy holding out the bottle is so close to me that we're almost touching. I can't see much of his face in the firelight, but something about him unnerves me. For the first time I understand what Mum means about people's energy. The thought of her is enough to make me reach out for the bottle. *You can keep your 'energy' and your self-actualisation, Mum.* This week is supposed to be about having fun. I feel the rough design down the square sides, like Braille for giants.

'Are you going to drink some or just fondle the bottle?' he says. He tucks his sand-coloured hair behind his ear. His voice belongs to Robert Redford in *Out Of Africa*.

I take a sip and work hard at not spitting it out.

'Easy,' he says. I take another, this time prepared for the feeling of liquid fire in my stomach, before handing the bottle back to him.

'Cool house,' I say, looking around.

'It's a straw house,' he replies, looking past me at the structure.

I can feel the tequila make its way around my body. 'Is that what the little piggy told you?'

He looks at me and laughs. His grin is boyish, as if the two of us are in on a joke. His eyes crinkle. I can tell immediately that he's older than us by the way he seems so comfortable in his body. 'The house is constructed of straw bales. Instead of bricks.'

'Oh,' I say and turn away. I hope that Theresa has seen this guy laughing with me.

The groups of people have become denser. Soon it will turn into one big crush of bodies. Someone changes the music, which causes an outcry. I scan the crowd, trying to guess the ages of everyone here. On the surface we all seem to wear the same uniform – guys in shorts and T-shirts; the girls in summer dresses and pretty much everyone in flip-flops. The main difference between the guys is the size of their bellies. The girls are easier to age, not by the way they dress but the way they stand. How have all these people appeared out of a seemingly deserted town?

'Are these all locals?' I ask the guy next to me. But he's in a conversation with somebody else, so I pretend I didn't say anything. I feel the signs of this turning into another of those crying in the corner parties, the way some people feel the beginnings of a migraine.

'Weekend locals,' answers the guy, turning back. He winks and hands me back the bottle of tequila.

SATURDAY

Even before I'm awake I know that something is wrong. The most appalling noise seems to throb through me. The pulse in my head is so strong that I can't open my eyes. It fills the room. It is as if the whole house is vibrating to it. It outlasts the possibility of being a low-flying plane or an earthquake or a passing apocalypse. When I am beginning to worry that it will shake our little stilted house loose, it disappears into nothing. But of course – the blasted train.

Light streams through the window above my head. It is startlingly bright, as if this little room is the sole receptor of the morning rays. Even the flimsy cream curtains shine. And it's suffering from a shortage of air. It is only when I try to sit up that I realise the throbbing in my head has nothing to do with the train. I look down and notice I'm in my T-shirt but nothing else. The pounding in my head steps up a gear but it's not a thought I care to explore until I've brushed my teeth and swallowed at least two painkillers.

The house is thick with sleep. On the passage wall opposite me is a mounted print of a topographical map of South Africa. It looks like the land is covered in an outbreak of angry acne. On the other side of their bedroom door, Louisa and Brett will be in bed. Louisa always sleeps coiled up in a tight ball. Well, she used to. I feel like an imposter stealing about, trying to make the bathroom door shut soundlessly.

I open the mirror-fronted medicine chest above the basin and leave it ajar. This is no time to have to face myself. My thoughts keep returning to last night, but I draw a worrying blank. Apart from tequila and being 'really fun'. What did I say, what did I do? It's fine for Louisa to get drunk because she simply gets louder and more fun. I, on the other hand – what could I have admitted about myself, and to whom? A shudder ripples through me. This is why I hardly ever let myself drink.

I remember masses of people and the guy with the tequila bottle. Oh dear – and dancing on a counter. Louisa's look of surprise, and telling her to loosen up.

If only I'd stuck to crying in a corner. A twist of dread wraps itself around my intestines. I will have made a fool of myself, and in front of Theresa and Helen. On the first night of our holiday. The thought makes me want to vomit. No doubt it will get back to Mum. Why do I do this? I am such an idiot. My breath feels shallow and snatched. If only I could get out of my head. The only thing that helps when I feel like this is running. Rory called it my 'literal escape mechanism'. *No shit.*

I pull my running clothes from my bag, fumble under my bed for my shoes and open the door. It's going to hurt, but

22

that's OK. At home I run in baggy track pants and a sweatshirt to avoid Mum's comments but here I pull on running shorts and a fleece. Back in the passage, I hesitate, caught by a nagging sensation that I'm forgetting something. *It's called a hangover*, I tell myself, *deal with it*.

In the kitchen I avoid looking at the counter littered with a half-eaten pizza and empty chip packets, and reach for the jug of cold water in the fridge. The shock of icy liquid rushing down into my stomach intensifies the throbbing in my skull. The sliding door is open. That's not clever. We may be halfway up the West Coast but this is still South Africa. And let's not forget about the baboons. Louisa teases me about the way I keep the doors locked even when we're home, but then we don't all get to live in high-walled, laser-protected houses in Constantia.

The fresh morning breeze pulls me closer and I start warming up my ankles as I walk towards the deck. This proves too coordinated a task and I grab onto the back of the sofa to stop myself tripping. This is when I see the boots. They are far too big to be Brett's. The black leather is scuffed to a charcoal grey, moulded to the feet that stepped out of them. They sit next to the sofa, side by side, winking at me. 'What?' I say. They know something I don't. I hurry on towards the deck, but come to an abrupt stop as I reach the door.

'*Told ya!*' gloat the black boots behind me. Leaning against the railing is a boy – correction, a man – wearing a navy jersey and what looks like my sarong. The heavy cloud of pain in my head bursts, like a whacked pinata, to reveal slices of lemon and big hands and me insisting on a game

23

of dare. 'This is not good,' I mutter. He keeps very still, as if he is concentrating on something out to sea, but the ocean is calm and empty this morning. As I watch, his right foot lazily rubs his left ankle. He stretches his shoulders, making a slight arch in his back, then returns to watching. I'm overwhelmed by a desire to walk up behind him and thread my arms around his waist, and also equally horrified at the thought. I cannot shake the sense that I have known that back and those arms. That I'd like to count the scars and freckles that litter them.

Tequila Guy turns around. 'Morning, sleepy,' he says and grins. He tucks a strand of hair behind his ear but it's too short and falls back into his face. 'How's that head?'

'Fine,' I say, nodding. 'Fine.' *For fuck's sake, Grace, say something else!* But my mind is empty of any other word. And I'm longing, aching to be on the beach. The only thing to do is make a run for it. I'm across the deck and halfway down the stairs before I manage a strangled 'Bye!' and a wave without looking back. I hear him reply, but can't make it out. At the top of the sandy path that leads to the beach, I turn back, shrug my shoulders and shake my head.

He speaks again.

I'm going to have to go back. 'What?' I call from a safe distance. I have to shield my face against the morning sun. 'I couldn't hear you. Spook.' His name leaves my lips of its own accord.

He rubs the back of his head. He looks down at me, a smile playing across his face. 'I said, "Have a good run."'

'Oh,' I say, backing away, 'OK.'

24

I stay close to the shoreline and pound out a rhythm into the sand. *Stu-pid bloo-dy i-di-ot.* Who is he? What is he doing here? I summon up all the indignation I have even though the answer is perfectly obvious.

I-di-ot. I-di-ot. The rhythm matches the pounding in my head. It feels as though I'm dragging weights attached to my legs but there is no option of stopping; he's probably watching. I pull off my fleece to allow the cool air to nip at me and chase me on.

I-di-ot. I-di-ot – as the distance between me and the deck grows I start to feel calmer. Then I remember challenging Spook to a game of darts. I told him I was a regional junior champion! I don't think they found my dart.

Ahead of me a freshwater stream carves a shallow path down the sand. I jump it, airborne for a second.

Sometimes when I run I picture a circus master, perched on a stool in the middle of a circus ring that sits inside the cavity of my stomach. The faster I run, the faster he spins, around and around. When I'm running properly, he spins without stopping. His outstretched whip is held perfectly straight by the momentum of his rotation, of my running. I cannot stop; it would see the whip come crashing down. But I'll never stop. The tip of the whip is millimetres short of the inside walls of my ribs. I feel it tickle the air between us. Faster and faster, so that now his red coat becomes a whirl, a smudge, and still I have more to give.

My lungs expand. As they fill with air they lift me, gently at first. I am free and wild. I am weightless. I can fly. I hold out my arms, and just for a second close my eyes.

25

Spook is stretched out on the sofa. His arms are folded across his chest, thumbs tucked into his armpits. He has a frayed leather bracelet around one wrist. Mercifully he appears to be sleeping. His body seems to fit the sofa perfectly, as though I am the stranger creeping up on him. At the same time, there is nothing strange about seeing him there. His familiarity makes me feel uneasy. I play with the idea of creeping around to the kitchen door to avoid having to walk past him. Oh my god, he's old! He must be at least thirty. This is bad. It's worse than the time I kissed the prison warder. At least that ended at the club.

'What happened to you?'

He's awake? Has he been watching me watching him? 'I fell.'

'Down a mountain?'

'Over some rocks.'

He raises an eyebrow. As I pass him, he reaches for my unhurt arm. 'You need to clean out those cuts.' His hand closes easily around it. The warm pressure makes me jump. I look down at the parallel lines that tear the skin where I'd tried to stop myself falling. Sand and dirt are lodged in the bloodied skin of my palms. The cuts, which I'd barely noticed, now start to sting unbearably. Tears mass threateningly behind my eyes.

'I'll be fine.' I'd made myself carry on after the fall. Otherwise it would have been a waste of a run.

'They need cleaning with Dettol or they'll get infected.'

'I don't think –'

But Spook is off the sofa. I'm staring at my sarong, which has come loose around his waist. I jerk my head away but not before I catch him grinning at me. Everything I do around him makes me feel stupid.

'I'll grab my kit from the car.'

Of course – the car. In my rush to get to the beach I must have missed it. The Toyota Cressida with the surfboard strapped to the roof and clothes scattered across the back seat. I feel blindsided by these disjointed images of last night. What else did I do? I sink into the sofa, still warm from his body. By the time he returns, I've started shivering.

'Shock,' he comments.

I suck in my breath as he starts dabbing at the cuts. It stings so much that I have to clench my bum not to say anything. I try to remove my hand, but his grip is too strong. He works methodically, ignoring my attempts to make him stop. As the silence stretches out, and the shock wears off, I begin to feel embarrassed. 'What kind of a name is Spook?'

He looks up. 'A nickname.' He drops one hand and starts on the other.

'Obviously,' I mutter.

'My old man gave it to me. I used to sleepwalk. My real name is Luke.'

'I prefer Luke,' I say.

'I prefer Spook.'

I bite the inside of my cheek and concentrate on the bookshelf across the room, picking out the Jo Nesbos and multiple copies of *Fifty Shades*, as well as what looks like the full set of Asterix. The two bottom shelves are stacked with puzzles and Monopoly and Risk, a few packs of cards bound together with elastic bands and a well-used Boggle set.

'Do you surf?' he asks.

'No.'

'I told your friend Brett I'd show him a surf site today.'

'You may regret it. He's probably the most accident-prone person you'll ever meet.'

Spook smiles. 'You all been friends for a while?'

I shrug. 'They're a couple now, obviously.'

Spook is trying to scrape loose a splinter of shell wedged into the gash in my palm. His fingernails are stubby.

I screw up my eyes.

'You have no meat on these poor bones. I thought I was going to break you last night,' he adds without looking up.

This takes my mind off my hand. *That's* what else happened. *Jesus, Grace!* More flashes, but still no solid memory.

Spook raises his eyes and looks at me. 'A guy likes a bit of padding.'

'Maybe you should stick to women your own age.'

Spook laughs. 'But if you remember it wasn't me doing the chasing.' He looks at me closely. 'You don't remember.'

I turn away, to find Louisa leaning against the wall, watching us. She is wearing sleeping shorts and a vest top. Her arms are crossed over her chest; she isn't wearing a bra.

'Morning, lovebirds,' she croons. I glance at Spook and catch him cringe slightly. Is that because of me? I yank my hand away and stand up, as if I've been caught doing something naughty.

'What did you do to my friend?' asks Louisa, seeing the first aid kit.

'Nothing! She threw herself over some rocks, apparently.'

'Hmm, she does that from time to time.'

I glare at Louisa in an 'I'm right here!' way but she's enjoying herself and won't catch my eye.

'If your friend ate a bit more she wouldn't need first aid every time she tripped.'

'Grace doesn't believe in eating. It's only us mortals who suffer from that need,' Louisa replies.

Spook packs away his Dettol kit and heads out the door.

I look at Louisa.

'What?' she says. 'I was being friendly.'

A noise, similar to that of an elephant stuck in a sculpture gallery, comes from the kitchen. A few moments later Brett appears holding a box of cereal. He is dressed in baggies and a T-shirt that looks as though he found it scrunched up in a hole in the ground. He loads his mouth with a handful of muesli and looks at me. 'Where's your dad, I mean boyfriend?'

I'm saved from having to reply by Spook coming back inside.

'Ready?' he says to Brett.

'Almost,' says Brett. He dumps the box on the table and walks out to the deck. 'Mother Ocean is calling. I'm coming, Sweet Lady, be gentle today!' he shouts.

He peers back inside with his wetsuit over his shoulder. 'Maybe we can pick up a crayfish on the way home.'

'Do you have a permit?' asks Spook.

'Nah.'

'Bro, don't you read the papers? You don't want to be caught with a mussel shell at the moment, let alone a crayfish.'

'You're getting old, dude. Fearful of life.' Brett shakes his head.

Spook laughs and steps into the waiting boots.

'What are you doing later?' Louisa asks him.

'No plans.' Spook empties his keys and scuffed wallet onto the table, then takes off his watch. It seems such a comfortable, 'at home' thing to do.

'Do you live around here?' I say.

'Nope.'

Louisa and I exchange a glance. 'So you're just here for the weekend?'

'Maybe.' He shrugs.

'Would you like to run a police check on him, or can we go surfing now?' says Brett from the door.

Spook laughs. 'Laters,' he says and follows Brett outside.

At the sound of Brett's car starting up I turn to Louisa. 'Does that mean he's going to hang around?'

'I thought you liked him.' Louisa shrugs.

'He must be at least thirty!'

Louisa turns back towards her bedroom. 'What was it you said last night? "Loosen up", Gracie! You only live once.' She looks back and flashes me an angelic smile.

I lie on my bed and listen to Louisa moving around in her bedroom, then the sound of the shower. My palms sting. I haven't fallen this badly since I was a little girl. Questions rush at me from the four corners of the empty room – what did I say to him last night? What exactly did we do? He's not my type. I like tall and lean, short dark hair. Mysteriously fucked up. Spook is way too straightforward to be attractive, but he has a nice smile. The other thing that I like about him is that he would totally freak Louisa's mother out. And my mum? The thought makes me laugh. Spook would make her shudder. He is the kind of guy my aunt Julia would fall head over heels in love with – she'd sell everything she owns, and follow him to Morocco.

Despite Louisa blaming Helen for us ending up in Baboon Point, it is actually down to her mother that we are here. For months Mrs Cele would not hear of an end-of-school week away. 'I didn't go away after school,' was her argument. This made Louisa roll her eyes and mutter, 'That's because you lived in a fucking hut!' under her breath.

Mrs Cele was obsessed with keeping Louisa away from Plettenberg Bay. She was convinced Louisa would spend a week accepting lifts from drugged-up drivers and having her drinks spiked, and return home a deflowered junkie. Little does she know Louisa's 'flower' has been potpourri for three years already, quite apart from the six-month-long lurve fest that's being going on with Brett. Louisa's mum is so much in denial about that relationship that Louisa and Brett can actually be messing around upstairs while she is downstairs in the kitchen. It would be unthinkable that Brett were anything other than Louisa's 'little friend'. Brett is not boyfriend material, he does not figure in the plan Mrs Cele has for Louisa's life. It's not only that he still looks weirdly pre-pubescent at the age of eighteen; his biggest fault is that he isn't 'going places'. I'm not going places either, but I don't pose the same threat to her daughter's future success.

Helen, on the other hand, is going straight into a business degree and a flat in Oranjezigt owned by her dad. Mrs Cele also

31

approves of Helen's big breasts and curves and is altogether too influenced by anything Helen says. As for Theresa – Mrs Cele refers to her as 'the Beauty Queen'. Whenever I'm at Louisa's house, Mrs Cele makes a point of asking after 'Helen and the Beauty Queen'.

When Helen told Mrs Cele she was going to her parents' house at Baboon Point instead of Plett, Louisa's mum sprang into action. Suddenly she had booked a house for us, 'prime position, right on the beach, so you can be near *all* your friends,' she beamed, looking at me out of the corner of her eye.

Louisa screamed at her for half an hour but at school the next day she announced that there was no way she was spending her first week of freedom being herded around Plett in parent-sponsored minivans or marquees complete with first-aiders and Christians handing out coffee.

Louisa sits down next to me, sipping from a mug. 'Let's go to Lambert's Bay.'

'Was I awful last night? I say, scratching at a blister of paint on the wall.

'Not awful, just, you know . . .'

No, I don't! I want to yell. *I don't remember a bloody thing.*

'Spook is probably a little surprised today. You were quite into him last night. You insisted on him coming back.' Louisa laughs. 'It was cute.'

I squeeze my eyes shut. After a while I sigh. 'Did you have a good time?' I turn over and look at her.

'I was looking after you.' Louisa hesitates. 'You gave Theresa a huge hug near the end, you know.'

'Jesus,' I mutter as I experience a whole new level of shame.

I feel Louisa bristle. 'I don't know why you're so hard on her.'

'How are we going to get to Lambert's Bay?' I ask to change the subject.

'We'll take Spook's car.' Louisa opens her hand and jingles the keys Spook dumped on the table.

I sit up. 'Are you sure? Stealing a car and underage driving? It's only Day One. We don't have to break every rule today.' We both know I'm simply playing for time. This is payback for last night.

'I know what I'm doing.'

The day has warmed up. Apart from a thin layer of white cloud above the horizon, the sky is clear. There is no wind today, which is unusual for this time of year. When a tourist site calls this area a 'kite-surfer's paradise', you know it's going to be windy. I think back to this morning, seeing Spook leaning against the railing; that horrible feeling of being surprised but not.

Louisa stops to lock the kitchen door.

I'm not convinced that stealing Spook's car for a joyride to the next town is such a great idea, but openly disagreeing with Louisa is pointless. Nothing puts her in a better mood than a loud argument. She always wins. 'The police will remain vigilant and on high alert at all times over this holiday season,' I read from the local paper I picked up in the cafe yesterday.

'That just means one of them is planning to turn up to work.' She leads the way down the stairs. 'I don't know who was worse last night – you or Brett.'

33

Her words are like that feeling of chewing on a mouth ulcer.

'Have you ever noticed at a certain point he becomes a maniac? Out of control.'

'He's eighteen, Lou.'

'One day he's going to hurt himself.'

'You sound like your mother.'

Already the overhanging Brazilian Pepper tree has dropped a light spray of its tiny white flowers on Spook's pale blue car. It looks alarmingly at home. The car has roof racks and a dent in the passenger door. Louisa unlocks the driver's door and gets inside.

'Do you remember sitting on Spook's lap as he drove home?'

'I did not!'

Louisa laughs. She is trying to pull the seat forward but it doesn't budge. She ends up sitting on the edge of it in order to reach the pedals. 'What is that smell?' She makes a face as she deposits the yellow wheel lock on the back seat.

I sniff. The car smells of damp clothes left in a pile for too long. 'We could go for a walk instead.'

There is a moment of wheel spinning and gravel spitting as Louisa attempts to reverse up the drive.

'Mother of God,' I mutter, grabbing the door handle.

'Turn on some music.'

The car radio is missing its removable face. I open the glove compartment to look for it, but there's nothing but a dog-eared logbook and a melted Kit Kat still in its wrapper. When I try to close the door, the catch won't hold. I bang it repeatedly. In the end I resort to resting my feet against it.

Louisa giggles. 'We can't steal the car and break it.' We set

34

off, jerking down the road. 'The clutch is crap,' says Louisa disdainfully. We pass the liquor store and the two tiny cafes.

'Where are the people?' shouts Louisa as we drive through the deserted streets. 'It's Saturday morning, where is everyone?'

'They've all gone to Lambert's Bay. Have you never been anywhere like this?' I ask.

'Never.'

'What about when you go and visit your grandmother?'

'That's different. There there's nothing but people. This town feels . . . forgotten.'

We make our way back to the road we turned off yesterday. A stream of cars and lorries guns past us. Louisa pulls up the handbrake but keeps revving in anticipation of a gap. 'I want something exciting to happen this week. Something more exciting than Plett.'

As soon as there is a tiny break in the cars, Louisa lurches forward but over-revs so that we stall halfway between the hard shoulder and the lane. A car swerves around us with its hooter blaring.

'Fuckwit!' shouts Louisa, as she restarts.

'Let's hope that wasn't an unmarked police car,' I say.

This is not my first visit to Lambert's Bay. There is a restaurant on the outskirts of town that my mum and her book club friends visit on their annual weekend away to see the spring flowers. Although I've managed to avoid being dragged along for the last few years, Lambert's Bay for me is synonymous with watching middle-aged women drinking gallons of red wine and discussing how awful men are. That, and the indescribably foul-smelling gannet nature reserve nearby.

Today the wide, flat streets are surprisingly busy. I don't remember much more than a few shops and the hub of activity around the harbour, but it seems that since I was last here the town has swelled back from the coastline. As we queue at an intersection, I compare the 'West Coast Real Estate' to the 'Cut Above' hair salon next door. The estate agency is empty – even the employee is outside leaning against the doorpost and smoking a cigarette; the hair salon is buzzing with Saturday morning customers. 'Back at home, you never think about these towns,' I say, thinking out loud. Or the people who populate them. All those dreams and heartbreaks that ultimately end in nothing.

'Why would you?' asks Louisa. Louisa's reaction makes me think about Rory. In Psychology Club he explained how drastically we under-utilise our brains. We are able to absorb every tiny detail of our surroundings, but filter out everything except what we want to see. Louisa's filter is very fine-tuned.

'There are all these parallel universes co-existing alongside ours that we never even consider.'

'Darling, you live in your very own parallel universe.'

We pull into the car park of a small shopping complex. It is littered with the usual self-appointed parking attendants. My mum always tips them because she's convinced otherwise they'd key our car. Today none of them even glance at Spook's car.

The complex has a bank, a Cash Converters, a liquor store and a Mr Price clothing store. Next to it is a Spar and a tiny shop called Surf Nation, although apart from a row of board shorts, it seems to cater exclusively to teenage girls. Louisa picks out a yellow maxi dress and disappears to the back to try it on. When she returns she's also holding a pair of denim hot pants. They're so short that the pockets stick out at the bottom.

'A present. You're the only person over ten years old in the world who should wear these.'

They make me feel cold just looking at them.

'Do you still see Mr Thomas?' she asks in a casual voice as she's paying.

For a moment I think I've imagined the question. We've never spoken about Rory until today. I wasn't even sure she knew about my weekly appointments. Instead of looking up, Louisa seems fascinated by the contents of her purse while she waits for me to answer.

'No,' I reply. I pick at the display of bead and string bracelets on the counter. Some of them are striped in reggae colours; others have little shells braided into the pattern. 'Why would I?'

Louisa shrugs. 'Theresa said –'

'Theresa doesn't know what she's talking about!'

From the surprise in Louisa's eyes, I realise my words came out too aggressively.

'OK,' she says quietly.

The silence is awful. It's the sound of the invisible stitching of our friendship beginning to tear. There are a hundred things that I know she wants me to tell her, but I said them all to Rory and look where that got me. 'Cheese and rice,' I say instead. *Jesus Christ.* Our Biology teacher – the man most unsuited in the world to teaching – used to mutter it regularly, especially when someone got a question wrong. It used to trigger unstoppable fit of giggles between us. It became our code for '*Oh my god, this is awkward*' moments, like the time when Louisa's mum recently asked us whether we thought any of the 'bad girls' in our year had had sex.

Louisa smiles without meeting my eye.

My first impression of Rory, or Mr Thomas, was that he was as big as a boulder, blocking out the sun. My headphones were in my ears so he seemed suddenly there, on the grass bank above me, standing legs apart, hands in his pockets.

I yanked the speakers from my ears and scrambled up from my seated position against the back wall of the swimming pool. 'Sir?' I blinked into the sunshine. No excuse in the world would make my being here acceptable, so I decided it was best not to say anything.

'Sorry to surprise you. I can't get down there. Done my back in.' As usual, he was wearing sweat pants and a school sweatshirt with 'Coach' written on the back. He oversaw boys' swimming and water polo. He also taught Geography and was the school guidance counsellor. Louisa thought it barbaric that we didn't have a female guidance counsellor and brought it up at every school council meeting.

'Any stray polo balls down there?'

'Nope.' I gathered my school bag, and stuffed my book and phone back inside.

'Nice spot.'

'It's never windy here,' I replied without thinking.

He waited for me to clamber up the side of the bank. 'Let's walk back together,' he said, in a pleasant voice I didn't trust. 'Grace, right? You've signed up for Psychology Club?'

I nodded. How could he have found me here? No one ever came here. It was my spot.

'You planning on studying Psychology at university?'

I nodded again.

'What topics would you like us to cover this term?' The previous week he had asked the same question during the first lunchtime meeting. Everyone else was bursting with questions.

I screwed up my eyes. 'How amputees can feel extreme pain in their limbs after they have been severed.'

'That's a good one. The brain is extraordinary.'

'My mum believes mood swings are nothing more than a chemical imbalance in the brain. So they're not even real. If you have half your brain removed, your personality changes.'

'If something feels real to you, then it's real.'

'That's so school counsellor-ish.'

He laughed. 'Well, it is my job. To give you a medical reason, I'd have to be a brain surgeon, in which case I wouldn't be renting a two-bedroom flat and driving a crappy car.'

The bell rang. 'Next time you're thinking of lurking behind the swimming pool, come and talk to me. I'm sure you have plenty more unanswerable questions for me to look foolish over.'

I looked down to hide a smile. 'I wasn't lurking.'

Early the next week I found myself in front of Mr Thomas's door. I raised my hand to knock, but the door wasn't properly closed so it swung open as I touched it. He was sitting behind the desk. In a seated position he seemed overweight rather than well built. He looked up as I was about to turn and run.

39

'Have you come up with another impossible question for me?'

I stepped inside and looked around the tiny office.

'It's ridiculously small, right? Obviously when they built the school in the 1950s there was no need for a guidance counsellor. Kids didn't have problems back then.'

I looked at him. 'When did the problems start?'

'With your generation,' he said.

I smiled and sat down.

He started talking. In this office, he wasn't Mr Thomas, he was Rory.

'Is that your real name?' I asked.

He looked surprised. 'Yes, why?'

'You don't look like a Rory. You look more like a Craig.'

'I wish you'd told my mother that.' He wanted to hear about my family.

'Just me and my mum.'

'No siblings? No dad?'

I shake my head. At Louisa's house there were always doors banging and relatives visiting and multiple phones ringing at the same time.

'Is she the Virgin Mary?'

I laughed. 'She acts like it.'

'What do you get up to on the weekend?'

Over the past few months I had been very busy trying to hide – from party invitations and Louisa, and especially my mother. 'Usual teenager stuff,' I replied with a shrug.

'Do you want to talk about eating?'

'Do *you* want to talk about eating?' I snapped back.

'I do. I love food, as you can see. Put anything down in front of me and I'll eat it. But curries! Nothing beats a curry. What about you?'

I stared at him. I didn't want to think about him eating.

'Sushi,' I replied.

He looked surprised.

'What?'

'I thought you'd be vegetarian or into one of those food routines that sounds more like a fraction – you know, "take your food, divide it in half, divide that portion in half and only eat on a day starting with T".'

I laughed and shook my head.

'That's a relief,' he replied, rubbing his hands together. 'In that case we'll get on well.'

Louisa is waiting for me at the Spar checkout counter. Her basket is groaning with variously packaged saturated fats. She frowns at her haul, mentally ticking things off as the cashier starts ringing them up. She points to the pack of one hundred paper plates. 'No more washing up. Wait –' She dashes away and arrives back with an armload of chips. 'Can't forget these!' she says. The cashier laughs. By the look of her she eats a lot of chips.

I look down into my basket of Coke Zero, skim milk, apples, carrots, celery and fat-free cream cheese. It was all I could find. The thin metal handles of the basket keep slipping over the cuts on my hand.

'I thought we could braai . . .' As Louisa is speaking she glances down into my basket. Her mouth draws a tight line.

'I don't mind braaiing,' I say.

'You're such a child,' she mutters.

'I beg your pardon?' I'm suddenly tired of the looks and bitten-back words. 'Do you want to say something?' I ask.

'It would only be to point out the obvious.'

'Which is?'

'You're on a death mission.'

'That's ridiculous.' A boy and his friend have come up behind us with a litre of Fanta and a bumper packet of Cheeseniks. Behind them a queue is beginning to form.

'OK. Eat this chocolate.' Louisa grabs a Tex bar from the rack next to the counter and shoves it under my nose.

I step backwards.

'Go on, eat it all, right here.'

I can feel the people behind us grow restless. It is so like Louisa to make a scene.

'I'll eat the chocolate,' offers one of the boys behind us.

'No one's eating the chocolate before it's paid for,' says the cashier quickly.

I glare at Louisa. 'You're picking a fight. You're trying to embarrass me.'

'Are you actually crazy? I am tired of being your mother!' shouts Louisa, waving the Tex bar. The cashier's eyes follow the chocolate.

'When did I ever ask you to be my mother?' I shout back. 'Last time I checked you were my friend.'

'Friend?' Louisa gapes at me. The chocolate falls onto the checkout counter. The cashier picks it up. 'The only time you are any fun is when you're so hammered you're falling over. "Oh Lou. I love you, I just want to be happy."' She mimics.

42

'Fuck you.' I dump my basket and walk out of the shop.

'*Yoooh!*' the cashier exclaims behind me. 'What's her problem?'

I don't wait for Louisa's reply. As I step outside the impact of the vibrant red Spar banner, the blue sky and the harsh sunlight make me feel dizzy. My cuts ache; my legs feel ready to give way. I reach out for one of the pillars at the entrance to steady myself. People pass me clutching shopping bags or pushing trolleys towards their cars. If Louisa and I had to meet now, I bet we wouldn't be friends.

'Sorry,' she says behind me.

I turn around. She's clutching the shopping bags; she's bought the stuff in my basket too. I'm about to hug her, then I remember her description of me last night. We've never had a touchy-feely friendship. Instead I manage a smile. 'Me too.'

'We're not going to get home unless we get some petrol,' I say, leaning over and looking at the red light flashing on the dashboard.

Louisa has taken an apple from one of the shopping bags and is holding it between her teeth as she starts the car. That apple is a whole meal. She's eating a meal on the way home.

We head up the main street. I try and block out the sound of the crunching apple. There is a makeshift market in a parking lot. It appears to specialise in fresh fish, plastic containers and children's clothes.

At the petrol station the attendant peers at us, his eyes taking in Louisa behind the steering wheel and me next to her. He says something to her in Xhosa.

She ignores him and says, 'One hundred rand of petrol please.'

He raises an eyebrow. A second later he is back. 'I need the key.'

'For what?' Louisa asks sharply.

'To open your petrol tank,' he replies, copying her accent.

'Oh,' says Louisa and hands Spook's bunch over.

When the attendant hands back the keys, he says, '*Sucha posh sisi with a buggard car.*'

He chuckles when she doesn't reply.

As we leave I say, 'He didn't wash the windscreen.'

'Would you, considering the state of this car?'

Louisa seems to be driving faster as we leave town. I turn to her, but she is frowning. She miscalculates the bend in the road and we end up swerving wildly away from the verge.

'Ever since I turned back onto the road there's been a car up my arse. When I speed up, it does too.'

The wobble in Louisa's voice scares me. She tries to change down, but can't find the correct gear. The engine surges like an asthmatic.

'It's probably the police,' I say. 'You'd better stop.'

'It's not the fucking police!' shouts Louisa.

I turn around. Behind us is a black Volkswagen Golf, with an Hermanus number plate. The car is so close that I can see the two people sitting in the front. They look like local fishermen. They are staring straight at us. The driver points at me. His face is stony. As well as being famous for pretty beaches and whales, Hermanus is home to many of the infamous poaching gangs that operate along that stretch of the East Coast. 'What do they want?' I glance at Louisa. Is this going to be the moment that the newspaper headlines become real? Carjackings happen every day. This is why people emigrate.

'I don't know, but there's no way I'm stopping,' replies Louisa.

'Just let them take the car!'

'It's not our fucking car!'

'They'll shoot us, Louisa!' The car speeds up to overtake. As it draws alongside, the passenger rolls down the window and shouts something. I can hear myself crying.

'Don't look at them!' barks Louisa.

A farm lorry is approaching in the opposite lane. There is not enough space for the three of us on the road. The lorry blares its horn.

Seconds before the lorry reaches us, the black car speeds ahead and disappears.

Louisa slows down and pulls over. She doesn't say anything but her hands are shaking. We sit, frozen, until the glove compartment falls open. We both stare at it but neither of us reacts.

I listen to Louisa's breath returning to normal. 'Right,' she says. 'You OK?'

'We should have gone to Plett,' I say, which makes her laugh.

'They were probably just some local weirdos.'

'D'you think?'

'Ja,' she says, but her voice sounds wobbly. 'Local joyriders mixing it up on a slow Saturday.'

'The car had a Hermanus registration. They weren't that local.'

'You know what I mean.' Louisa sounds exasperated.

On the way back we find ourselves on a dirt road. The car judders along. It feels as if a particularly big jolt could make it simply fall apart. Neither of us says anything else about the black car, but as we turn into our road, Louisa slows to a crawl. 'There is no reason to mention that black car to the boys. It was nothing, OK?'

I know that Louisa is more worried about Brett's reaction than Spook's. She hates showing any sign of vulnerability. 'OK,' I reply.

Brett's car is parked under the tree. Louisa jerks to a stop behind it and curses, but whether this is at the crappy clutch or that Spook will know we took his car, I'm not sure.

I help her gather the shopping bags from the back seat and follow her up the stairs to the deck. She bristles at the sound of Spook's voice.

Louisa is incapable of apologising. She stalks past the boys and into the house. Spook is shirtless, standing over an upside-down surfboard on the table. He has a tattoo between his shoulder blades. It is of two heartbeats. Instead of the usually straight line between them, the heartbeats are connected by three curly waves, the same pattern as I drew on the car window. He looks up at Louisa but doesn't comment.

'Why are you back so soon?' I ask.

'No waves,' replies Brett, lying back in a deck chair with his eyes closed.

'There were waves,' says Spook, 'just none big enough for Kelly Slater here.'

'Bru, I'm not going to waste my time splashing around in a millpond. There is beer to be drunk. Parties to be partied.'

Spook raises an eyebrow.

Brett yawns expansively and stretches before flumping back into the same position. 'You left your phone behind. I had a lovely chat with your mum,' he says to me.

'What did you say?' My mother loves Brett the way one does an exotic monkey.

'I told her that now I'm eighteen she and I can explore our mutual passion without any shame.'

'Brett?'

'She said, "Brett Taylor, you're a scream!" I like the way she says "Brett Taylor". It reduces the years between us.' He makes a revolting sound against his hand.

'Anything else?' I ask.

'Oh yes. She said "Tell Grace that if she doesn't phone me back, I'm coming up to Baboon Point myself."' He turns to Spook. 'You could have mother *and* daughter!'

'Don't be disgusting!' I screw up my face.

Spook laughs. 'That never turns out well.'

Louisa reappears, in the new yellow dress, with a six-pack of beer and a packet of chips. Balsamic vinegar flavour – the best. Spook looks up at her. I can see in his glance that he's annoyed.

She flips the lid off a bottle and hands it to Spook.

Spook inclines his head and takes a sip. 'Do you often nick strangers' cars?'

I look at Louisa.

'Do you often stay over at strangers' houses?' she replies.

'That car is my livelihood.'

'I put one hundred rand's worth of petrol in it,' comments Louisa and has a sip of beer. 'One more thing –'

She's going to tell him about the black Golf.

'I couldn't open the boot but I swear to God that wasn't my fault.' Louisa leans back into a chair and rests her blue-tipped toes against the railing. I look at her but she is still bristling and won't catch my eye. Spook has that quasi-relaxed look which only an idiot would take at face value.

We've never had a set of rules at home. I suppose they are obsolete when there are only two of you. The thing I learnt very early on was that as far as the rest of the world is concerned, the two of us are always 'fine'. Every telephone conversation my mum has begins with 'Yup, we're fine, thanks. Grace is fine. Work's fine.' It is a huge, protective boulder of a word to hide behind.

Me being fine all the time really bothered Rory. 'What would happen if you weren't *fine*?' he asked. He was so easy to read. He was always looking out for a trauma that would make sense of why I'm me. No trauma, Rory. Simply the view that if we all said how we truly feel, life would be chaotic. What is grossly unfair is that while I'm making the effort to be 'fine' at all costs, most other people seem unaffected by contrary emotions openly clashing against each other. It is as though they were born with an extra layer of skin.

'Well then,' says Brett, rubbing his hands together, 'let's get drunk!'

My cuts ache. I hate the open packet of chips on the table. I hate Louisa for the silence. All the oxygen seems to have been sucked out of the afternoon. I have to get away.

Back in my room I start tidying. Spook's belongings lie scattered about, like a dog spraying its territory. My hunger makes me feel restless and out of control. At school I used to look forward to my grumbling stomach. It meant that another day was going according to plan. But here there is no plan. The rest of my life has no plan. I notice that my hands are shaking; it seems my brain is no longer able to control the extremities of my body. The combination of the car and the fall on the beach and waking up, apparently having slept with a complete stranger, is too much. I try to fold Spook's jeans, but end up dropping them. A passport-sized, dark green book slips out of the back pocket onto the floor. It's curved to the shape of Spook's bum. It's an ID document with the old South African emblem in faded gold. I lean over for it. The plastic cover is torn and studded with trapped sand.

Spook is behind me. I'm stupidly holding the book in one hand and the jeans in my other. He leans over me and takes the ID book from my hand. His stubbly cheek is inches away from mine. 'My old lady.' he says, his voice gruff. He opens it and a trickle of sand falls to the floor. I lean over and look at the picture. The black and white photo of a woman is faded to the point that any similarities to Spook are blurred. Her name is Cornelia Roux.

I feel shocked by this unexpected vulnerability – it belongs to a child, not a fully grown man. Instead of saying anything I hold out the pair of jeans.

'She left it behind the day she walked out.' He's still looking at the picture. 'For the longest time I thought she'd come back for it. I thought she'd left it behind on purpose.'

'Don't you have any other pictures of her?' I say. My embarrassment makes the question sound rude. Having sex with someone does not oblige him to confide in you, especially when he is nearly twice your age and should be married and settled down.

'Of course.' He laughs as though I'm the weird one. But when I look at him, his eyes are tender and I want to reach out and stroke his cheek and suddenly he's looking at me and I know he can read my thoughts. He teases out the moment; then leans forward and plants the gentlest kiss on my lips, and leaves the room.

Two hundred sit-ups later I feel calmer. As I'm having a shower to get rid of my red face, I decide that maybe the tension between Spook and Louisa is a good thing. He needs to go. Everything about him, from the way he has just appeared without warning, to the way that whenever he is around it is as though every cell in my body is on high alert, makes me feel out of control.

On my way outside I grab two carrots from the fridge. Music floats through the house. Outside, Spook is bent over the braai. He makes a comment to Louisa, which makes Brett laugh. I hesitate in the sitting room, trying to catch up with the change in mood. This isn't supposed to be happening – Spook should be on the verge of leaving, not cooking lunch.

Louisa is sitting at the table, bent over an open newspaper. She looks up. 'Listen to this, this is unbelievable: "Abalone poaching syndicate harvest abalone worth more than R2 billion and pocket more than R50 million."'

Brett groans. 'She's off again.'

Poaching is one of those topics I have a 'headline' knowledge of. I know it's to do with the government and unemployment in the local communities, which means that fishermen resort to illegal poaching . . . which in turn has had an environmental impact on the coastline. And of course I know that gangs make money out of poaching, but that's about it. I try not to get involved in Louisa's heated debates as she always knows more than me and I end up feeling foolish. It was the same a few months ago when my mum and my aunt Julia had a loud argument about poachers.

Louisa's still reading aloud, she hasn't noticed me in the doorway. 'It says here that this particular syndicate has been operating since at least 1986 but have been very hard to catch. That's twenty-seven years! The whole thing is like a multi-national business, employing spotters, packers, drivers, collectors of money, divers and poachers, obviously.'

'Not to mention the police,' says Brett.

'Exactly. What kind of a police force takes twenty-seven years to crack down on a syndicate? Your precious "Mother Ocean" is just another rape victim in this country, Brett.'

Spook chokes on his mouthful of beer.

'Welcome to life with Louisa,' says Brett to Spook. 'It's never dull.'

* * *

It was over Sunday lunch; Julia's weekly meal with us and the most argumentative three hours of the week. Ju-Ju claimed poaching was another legacy of apartheid and the continuing staggering unemployment. Her argument was that if the Minister of Fisheries would open up the coastline and curb the power of the huge fishing companies, local fishermen could make a decent living from the sea and we wouldn't have a poaching problem.

'Bullshit, Julia,' Mum said. 'It's a lucrative, highly organised criminal operation. And the ringleaders don't give a shit. They plunder the coastline to make themselves rich. They're pushing *tik** in the playgrounds and spreading cold-blooded terror.' As with most of their conversations, it wasn't the poachers they were arguing about. It was the type of argument that ended with one of them saying: 'I can't help it if that's the way you choose to see the world.'

'What I don't understand is the connection between tik and abalone,' I comment, a question I didn't have the energy to ask my mum as it would simply have drawn out the argument with Ju-Ju.

'Where have you been?' Louisa glances up.

'Having a shower,' I mumble.

She raises an eyebrow as she takes a sip of beer. 'The gangs trade the abalone, mainly to the Far East, in exchange for the chemicals used to produce tik. So they control the abalone and the local drug trade.'

'Jeez, tik is scary shit. My mum has a friend whose cousin was sitting down to supper with her family one Saturday night and two guys jumped over their wall. When the

* A street version of crystal meth manufactured locally

husband tried to defend his family against the guys, they shot him in the eye.'

'Brett, that's horrible!' I scrunch up my face.

'It's true. They shot him in front of his kids. They were off their faces on tik.'

'So how would you fix the poaching problem, madame President?' I ask Louisa.

'Incentivise the communities to stand up to the gangs,' replies Louisa without hesitation. How does she manage to have an answer to everything?

'How?' I reply.

Louisa flashes me her million-dollar smile, which is a sure sign she's winging it. 'Chocolates. Tex bars. No one can resist a Tex bar, right?'

I pull a face at her and turn to Spook. He has been silent all this time. 'What do you think about poaching?'

Spook looks out towards the ocean then back at me. 'I think I should get some more beers,' he says and gathers the empty bottles on the table.

'Spook has been telling us about his surfing trips to "Indo".' Louisa air-quotes with heavy sarcasm.

'It sounds flipping awesome,' says Brett. He's leaning against the railing. He turns and looks out over the ocean. 'So many flipping *awesome* places to go.' His voice is charged with an urgency that makes Louisa look up.

I glance after Spook, despite myself. Even after two hundred sit-ups I can still feel his kiss.

Louisa's phone rings. She picks it up. 'It's Helen,' she says – in a tone that could easily be taken as relief – and disappears inside.

The afternoon sun has passed overhead and is now slipping heavily towards the horizon. The remains of our lunch are spread out on the table. The fat from the lamb chops in the pan has congealed into mini oil slicks. The potatoes in the salad have grown a crust. As the empty beer bottles have piled up, so a tension between Spook and Louisa has crept back into the conversation.

'I'm not saying a gap year is a bad thing, of course Brett should go and have a good time, but university is important,' Louisa says to Spook.

'What if you don't want to go to university?' Spook asks mildly.

'Everyone wants to go to university,' Louisa snaps.

Brett hasn't said anything for a while. Now he stands up a little unsteadily and turns towards the sea. 'Oh look, it's about time for sundowners,' he says.

'What are you set to study?' Spook continues with Louisa, undaunted by her tone.

'Social work,' she says, with a little look at Brett and me.

'Wow!' says Spook.

'Wow what?'

'I would have put you down as a lawyer. You don't strike me as a person who oozes with compassion.'

'I ooze when the situation calls for it,' replies Louisa.

Spook laughs. 'What about you?' He turns to me. The question catches me off guard. Leftover food crowds my vision. It is messy and unhygienic. I turn away from it and try to focus on Spook's question. My mum was training to be an opera

'You guys don't strike me as West Coast people,' Spook says in the evening gloom. There is a rhythmic thud of music in the distance as Saturday night parties begin to warm up. Someone on our road is braaiing.

Louisa has just inhaled and starts laughing. 'No,' she says. 'We wanted to go to Plett or Hermanus. Then my mother got involved. This is her idea of a compromise.'

Spook raises an eyebrow.

'Funny, right? I can almost hear my mum laughing. We couldn't get into trouble here even if we paid for it. Why are you here?' asks Louisa as she hands me the joint. I get up without taking a drag and pass it to Brett.

'This particular stretch of ocean is my playground,' he says. 'There is a break that I would happily spend the rest of my life surfing. I am its devotee.'

Brett snorts on the joint. 'Dude, come on.'

Spook relights the joint and takes another drag. 'I guess that sounds stupid when you're eighteen. But surfing isn't a *sport* for me. The ocean is my therapist and my guru all rolled into one.'

'Funny,' says Brett.

'Hey?'

'Rolled, as in rolling waves. I thought you were making a joke.'

Spook looks at him. 'No. For kids these days it's all about tricks and moves on the board and belonging to the cool club. A few years ago I brought a longboard up here. The first time you get the hang of it, it's like you're suddenly surfing alongside the spirits of August and Hynson.'

57

'Oh please, you're as much part of a club as *kids these days*,' Louisa says, air-quoting Spook.

'Where is the club? Mine is a soul journey, a commitment to the water that transcends everything else.'

Spook's words make me cringe; I wish he hadn't said them. They sound clunky in the soft light.

'That doesn't sound transcendent; that sounds emotionally retarded!' replies Louisa. I smile. I'd forgotten how aggro dope makes her.

Spook laughs. 'Every day you go out on your board, you face yourself. Most people spend their lives running from that experience.'

'If I get anywhere close to the soul shit, you have my full permission to exterminate me,' says Brett to Louisa.

Spook laughs. He fiddles with the pack of Rizlas. 'We all start out looking for a good time, to screw birds, to live the dream. But at some point you realise that that's not enough.'

I blush, despite myself. I feel Louisa looking at me. She knows me too well. 'Must be tough on the person who falls in love with you,' she comments.

I glare at her.

'Why?' Spook laughs.

'It's such a selfish existence.'

'I'm no more selfish than all my mates who've bought a home and have a wifey and kids and spend Saturday afternoons watching rugby with their buddies. That's cool, man, I'm not judging. But we're all selfish.' For a moment he wanders off into a stoned thought, then suddenly he's back. '"Man was born free, and he is everywhere in chains."'

'Did you just make that up?' asks Brett.

Spook laughs. 'It's fucking Rousseau, man. Society wants you to follow the norm like little sheep because if you don't, all the other little sheepies feel insecure.' Spook rubs the back of his head. 'Well, fuck them.'

Louisa laughs. 'That's all very well when you're young, but you'll end up a sad, lonely old man with skin cancer.'

'No he won't, he'll be a legend,' says Brett.

Louisa sends Brett a sharp look.

'I'm not sure I even want to reach old man status.'

'How very rock and roll,' snaps Louisa.

Spook laughs. 'They call it a rat race for a reason. All you have to do is step away and you're free.'

'To live in a car,' says Louisa.

I envy Louisa. She wants that life of happy families and a house with a pool. She doesn't realise it, but she has a sense of entitlement, a birthright into that world. Brett is part of that world too, even though he's enjoying rebelling against it at the moment. I've never felt that. I'm not sure I want it. The problem is I don't know what else to do, how else to be. I don't want to be my mother, always on the edges of that world, even though she chose to defy it. Spook seems to have made up his own world.

Louisa stands in front of Brett and cups his face. 'Come down to the beach with me.'

'Why?'

'Come,' says Louisa, in that growly tigress voice she gets from nowhere.

Louisa and Brett disappearing into the evening leaves Spook and me alone. Did she do this on purpose? My hands feel clammy. The kiss earlier, so light and perfect, now feels laden with expectation. If this were a film, I'd glance up to find Spook looking at me. He'd tuck his hair behind his ear. I would smile and there would be a cute moment when we realise we're reading each other's thoughts. Then the look would grow into something more. Of course that doesn't happen – after all, if it were a film that would make me the main character and there'd never be a film about me.

Desperate to break the silence, I blurt out: 'Do you really believe all that stuff?'

Spook looks surprised. 'Sure.'

'It sounds so surfy.'

'I don't care what it sounds like.' He stretches lazily then sits up with a decisive sniff. 'I'm going to head to the hotel for a drink. Do you want to come along?'

What? We're supposed to be having sex! At the very least he's supposed to want to. 'Nah,' I manage to reply in the end.

He looks at me. 'You remind me of someone I once knew.'

I raise an eyebrow.

'A little minx of a girl.'

'Doesn't sound like me.'

He laughs.

'What happened to her?'

'Dunno. She got married, had kids. What happens to everyone?'

'She could have died. It would be more of a story.'

Spook frowns at me then bursts out laughing. 'I like you,' he says. He gets up and steps into his boots. 'Take it easy.'

* * *

60

Spook has taken the last of the evening sun and left me in the gloom. Why did he say 'take it easy'? Am I coming across as stressed? I thought I was doing well considering the afternoon of out-staring uneaten food. Still, I must be the only eighteen-year-old in the world who would choose to sit outside on a deck alone on a Saturday night instead of going out and having a good time.

Rory was a man of quotes. I was impressed until he started reusing them. One of the all-time favourites he would pull out was 'What is most personal is most universal'. Thinking of it now makes me laugh. Shows how much you know, Rory. I get up quickly. I am not going to sit alone outside and think about his nuggets of wisdom.

The empty sitting room feels full of departed voices. How can you choose to be alone one minute and truly hate it the next? I switch on a standing lamp near the sofa and lean across the coffee table for a pack of cards. Solitaire. The cards hurt the cuts on my palm. It's a crap round. I think about cheating, but what would be the point? It looks very dark outside. There are no streetlights. Is this a conscious hippy-organic decision by the residents? It's far more likely that no one's bothered to fill out the streetlight application form. Spook has left his jersey behind. I pick it up and sniff it, expecting a smoky, sweaty smell, but find none. 'Huh,' I say. I like jerseys. I put it on and tug the sleeves over my wrists. It feels as if I've crawled into a cocoon.

This is the kind of night that needs opera. 'Dido's Lament' from *Dido and Aeneas* to be specific. Dido rejects Aeneas for having thought of leaving her but is so heartbroken that she decides to die. It's very beautiful. Opera is the only thing in the world big enough to hold all emotion. It is bigger than the deepest despair or most frivolous fantasies. You can hide in it.

Despite being definitely 'fine' all the time, if Mum gets home and blasts opera through the house, I know to leave her for a while. If she puts on anything by Wagner, I may end up having to cook my own supper. For as long as I can remember, Mum has dragged me to every operatic staging at Artscape, 'pitifully few that they are'. Even though I'd simply curl up and go to sleep next to her, it was always me she took along. Yet despite the fact that she was training to become an opera singer, she doesn't sing. Sometimes I think she stopped singing the day she got pregnant. I once asked her why she didn't name me Dido or Carmen or Violetta or Isolde. 'They're all so tragic,' she smiled. *We are not tragic – we are fine.*

I could have done with an unusual name like Isolde – instead she gave me a little old lady's name, after a singer so obscure it in itself is tragic. Gracie Fields. Wartime entertainer of troops and general cat's chorister. I've never understood Mum's devotion to Gracie Fields, but it has something to do with the Christopher Robin song. This was the only song Mum ever sang to me. She sang every night as she tucked me up. It never ceased to thrill me how such a deep, rich voice came from her small body. It would make my scalp tingle. I used to wonder where she kept it for the rest of the day. She'd sit on the side of my bed, scoop her long hair, twist it around her finger a few times, and begin. 'Hush, hush, whisper who dares, Christopher Robin is saying his prayers.'

That was a long time ago. Nowadays it's all frown lines and that forced bright tone. Until the night before we left. I was in the kitchen when she got home from yoga. I'd been packing for our week away, trying to find some jeans that would fit. Right at the back of the cupboard I'd pulled out my favourite jeans of all time.

She dumped two bags of food on the counter. I helped her unpack, looking out for anything I could take on the holiday.

'I've joined a choir,' she said as she opened the fridge and poured herself a glass of wine.

I frowned. I had a bag of carrots and some fat-free yoghurt. 'But you've always only sung to me.'

Mum's face softened, which made me wish I hadn't said that. 'You outgrew my singing a while ago.'

Still, for some reason I felt uneasy. Even wanting to join a choir seemed distinctly out of character for Mum. It was the kind of thing Theresa's mum Janey would encourage her to do. 'Wow. A choir. That's very hip.'

'I think so,' she agreed, happily ignoring my sarcasm. She was about to walk out the kitchen when she stopped. 'Are those the jeans I got you from Gap?' Her tone was of someone coming across a long-forgotten photo.

I looked down and without thinking answered, 'Yup.'

When she spoke again, her voice had changed. It was small and worried, like a child who doesn't understand. 'But we got those when you were twelve.'

Shit. 'They're very stretchy,' I said and left the kitchen.

From my bedroom I listened to her walking around the house, up and down, as if she was looking for something.

Then she was at my door. Her body was rigid underneath her yoga pants and sweatshirt. 'For the last six months I have been walking on eggshells around you. No more.' Mum doesn't shout. The angrier she is, the quieter her voice gets. Her words came out clear and dangerously measured. 'I want you to think very carefully this week about what it is you're trying to achieve. Because the way I see it, you're stringing us all along in a very elaborate game.'

'What game?'

'I am not finished. I will support and love you through whatever it is that is causing you anxiety but I will not follow you down this road of self-destruction. If you insist on continuing like this, Grace, I'm afraid we are not on the same team.'

'What's that supposed to mean?'

Mum took a deep breath. 'It means that you *will* attend the three-month outpatients' programme. If that doesn't help we'll try something else.'

I looked up at her. 'What about varsity?'

Mum shook her head. 'That will have to wait.'

I felt my mouth drop open. I laughed. Ninety-five percent of me was convinced she'd never be that cruel. 'You don't have the right to decide that.'

Mum seemed to grow taller. 'Yes, Grace, I do.'

'That course is the one good thing in my life and you're going to take that away? I won't go to that stupid place. I'd rather die.'

Mum's pupils contracted. For the first time I seemed to have rattled her. 'You don't mean that,' she said and left the room.

I shake away the memory and Mum's words. She's just trying to scare me. But I'm stronger than she thinks. I won't answer her calls and I won't go on any programme.

At the sound of Louisa and Brett returning I get up quickly and slip away to my room. Somewhere at the back of my mind I know I should take the jersey off, but it's too warm. It would be like peeling off a layer of skin.

SUNDAY

Spook is leaning over me, shaking my shoulder gently. He's switched the bedside lamp on; it feels like the middle of the night.

I sit up, groggy. 'What?'

'Get dressed,' he whispers and leaves the room.

When he returns with a mug of tea, I haven't yet made it out of bed. He looks at me and I suddenly remember I'm still wearing his jersey.

'Outside. Five minutes. Put your costume on and dress warmly.'

It is not yet light. The air is sharp and salty. The waking birds are the only indication that dawn is approaching. I grasp the mug of tea and shiver in my track pants and sweatshirt. 'Are you crazy?'

'Let's go,' he replies.

'Spook, it's dark.' But I follow him nonetheless down to the car. He has two boards strapped to the roof-rack and is bundling wetsuits onto the back seat.

'Jump in,' he says cheerfully.

Spook drives quickly through the sleeping streets. The sky is lightening into a purpley blue.

'Where are we going?'

He rubs the back of his head and grins at me. 'Church.'

'What? With surfboards?'

He laughs.

'Do you belong to some freaky sect?'

He shrugs. 'Some people think so.'

I've been abducted by a madman.

He looks over at me. 'Relax, the first time is always the best.'

We leave Baboon Point and follow the dirt road Louisa and I drove back on from Lambert's Bay. I'm about to demand to know more, but suddenly the train is approaching, a great dark hulk looming through the pre-dawn haze. It speeds by, metres from my side of the car, the sound deafening. 'Jeez,' I say as the endless line of cargo carriages charges past, 'why put a track through the middle of a seaside village?'

'The train was here first.'

'It's ugly.'

Spook finds this funny. 'It's delivering iron ore from the Northern Cape to Saldanha. Three hundred and forty-two carriages, each carrying one hundred tonnes of ore. You'll see the tankers lining up on the horizon, waiting to collect it.'

'It's still ugly.'

'Capitalism is ugly. You can walk along the tracks all the way up to the tunnel that goes through Baboon Point.'

'Have you been in there?'

'Sure.'

'At the same time as a train?'

Spook frowns at me. 'You really do have a death wish.'

Being back on this road reminds me of the black car yesterday. The memory of those two men's menacing expressions, as if they were delivering a message. Should I tell Spook, despite what Louisa said? But what if he laughs at me?

The sky is brightening, revealing the world in sleepy colours. I don't want to ruin it by bringing up us taking his car again.

Spook pulls over on the side of the road and jumps out. I look over the deserted beach, wondering why the hell I agreed to this, when he opens my door and chucks me Brett's second skin and wetsuit. 'That guy has got enough kit to open a surf shop,' he remarks, holding what looks like a rubber balaclava and booties.

'Uh, Spook – I don't surf.'

'Good, 'cos it's a lake out there this morning.' He watches me, but there is no way I'm undressing in front of him. The thought of walking around in a wetsuit in front of him is bad enough. As if he suddenly understands, he drops the kit and walks away.

'If I get hypothermia, I'm blaming you,' I call, as I'm hopping on one leg, struggling to pull the suit on. What if it's too small?

'It helps to wee,' he says, returning with his suit on up to his waist.

'What?' I ask as he zips me up.

69

'It warms the suit up,' he replies, fitting the rubber balaclava over my head. Our faces are inches apart. His face looks younger in the soft light; his greenish eyes have brown flecks in them.

'I'm going to pretend you didn't say that,' I reply.

Spook carries both boards across the white sand to the water's edge. His body seems more athletic in a wetsuit; he has beautifully shaped legs. But his stomach sticks out like a pregnant bump. He hands me Brett's board. 'Got it?' he asks.

Of course not! I want to shout, *I don't get anything about this*. But I smile.

'Follow me.' After a few strides, Spook launches himself onto his board and starts paddling. The board is surprisingly heavy. I take a few tentative steps forward and almost topple over. Despite the suit, the freezing water takes my breath away. For a while all I can do is gasp repeatedly. It takes every ounce of bloody-minded determination to keep me from turning around and making for the car. The board is heavy and awkward in the water. I try to copy him as best I can by lying on the board, but despite the wax I slip about, like a soaped-up seal. The apparently flat sea shoots up at me, dumping water into my face and stinging my eyes.

He looks back at me. 'Paddle.'

My hands burn from the cold. The next time he looks back I've fallen off. I'm so cold I can't even cry. My head aches. He comes back alongside, gets off his board and stands in front of mine to steady it. 'Relax,' he says.

I make a face at him. 'The waves keep knocking me off,' I say through chattering teeth. 'Why am I doing this?'

Spook laughs loudly. 'There are no waves. It's unnaturally flat this morning. And you're doing it because it's magic.'

'This reminds me of that scene in *Titanic*, you know, where Leonardo Di Caprio dies of cold and sinks to the bottom of the sea?'

He grins. 'I'm not that good-looking.'

He walks alongside, holding the board. 'See – no more "waves". OK?' I nod, out of humiliation more than anything. 'Let's go.' He returns to his board, graceful as a dancer. Now that I'm steady, I find the rhythm and paddle behind him. After a few minutes he sits up on his board. When I catch up, he reaches out and takes hold of mine.

'Now what?' I ask, as I clamber into a sitting position.

'Nothing. Now we sit.'

'You're joking.' I've lost all feeling in my feet. The rest of my body is shaking. 'A shark could have bitten my legs off and I would have no idea.'

'Shhh,' he replies.

I look around. The horizon is backlit with an orangey-pink layer. The rest of the sky is a hazy yellow. The quiet makes me nervous.

'Stop wriggling,' he says.

I sit next to him on Brett's board. 'Where are the waves?'

'The swell hasn't pulled in yet.'

'It's peaceful,' I comment. Apart from the bobbing kelp in the water nearby that looks horribly similar to seals. Or worse.

'Do you feel it?' he says. 'It's epic.'

I try, but I feel coerced, like when I get trapped in one of Mum's meditation sessions at home. 'It's difficult to tap into the majesty when I keep feeling things touching my legs,' I say.

'Put your feet up. I've got you.'

I glance at him. His eyes are big and genuine, so I do as he says. 'We're drifting,' I say after a moment.

'It's cool,' he replies. 'Close your eyes.'

I hear gulls that I hadn't noticed before and the water lapping. It's gently shifting us all the time, almost like rocking. Spook's firm hold on the board is like being adrift and moored at the same time. The smell of kelp and salt wash through me. I am intensely aware of how cold every cell in my body is.

When I open my eyes, he is smiling at me. 'It is kind of like church, huh?' He pulls my board closer and takes hold of my hand. The beach is deserted. The small curve of white sand is bordered on each side by flat rocks. 'No better place on earth than this coast.' Spook's voice is soft. 'Look at those hills in the distance; in this light they're almost . . . tender.'

Watching him, I catch a glimpse of both the very small boy he was and who he'll become as an old man. In the water, in his element, Spook becomes almost mythical.

'The one thing that Muizenberg has that this coast doesn't is great coffee,' I comment on the way back up the sand.

'Balls,' Spook replies. His face is still glowing, and he shakes the water out of his hair like a dog.

Once I'm back in my clothes and not shaking quite so violently, I go and find him at the back of the car. 'I thought Louisa said the boot was broken.'

'Call it kiddie-locked,' he replies.

He has set up a gas canister and a small coffee roasting pot. Out of a crate in the boot he lifts a bag of coffee beans and a grinder. 'Seriously?' I say, leaning over his kit.

'Third best thing in the world is fresh coffee,' he replies. My heart skips at his words, but I'm too shy to take him up on them. Instead I watch him work, his brow slightly creased in concentration.

'You've got it all figured out,' I comment.

He looks up. 'Nah, I just know what I like.' He holds my gaze until I blush and look away. I wander down to a rock. The sky is a fresh morning blue, the ocean is resting, playing sleepily with the morning light that bounces off it. The only sounds are those of Spook whistling tunelessly behind me and the indistinct hum of a coastline waking up. Our footprints are the only ones to mark the white sand – it could be the first day of the world. For the first time in my life I feel like there is a chink of light, another way. Spook's world is raw, cut down to what matters. He is the first person I've met who seems free.

Spook sits down next to me with two steaming mugs. When he hands me one, my heart drops. 'I should have said – I don't drink condensed milk.' Once upon a time it was my favourite thing in the world; there was always a can in my Christmas stocking. Louisa and I used to buy tins of it, punch two holes in the top and carry it around in our school bags. Sipping at it was the only way to survive Chemistry. When did we stop doing that? Last year, sometime between Louisa's watermelon diet and our decision to only eat green things.

'Everyone likes condensed milk,' Spook scoffs.

'No.' I shake my head vigorously, feeling panic rising. 'It's just –'

'What?' he asks, his bush-coloured eyes challenging. 'I dare you.'

I take a sip of the most delicious coffee in the world. I hold the mug near my lips a moment, devouring the smell, then put it down on the rock. 'I just don't like sweet coffee.'

I feel Spook studying me for a moment. Then he reaches out and rubs my back. The tenderness of the action makes me want to climb into his lap and howl but instead I straighten up and smile. 'When did you learn to surf?'

He gives my shoulders a gentle squeeze. 'I was surfing as soon as I could carry a board.' He drains the last of his coffee. 'Never much going on at home so I was always down at Bayworld.' He laughs at the memory. 'There were about six of us *laaitjies** there. Causing mayhem at every opportunity.'

I can imagine him with his blonde hair and surfer's attitude. He and his friends would be the type of boys who hang about at the top of the beach and laugh loudly every time you walk past. He wouldn't give me a second glance if he were eighteen now.

Seagulls overhead break the silence. The sound triggers an inexplicable sense that I've been expecting this moment. Something has prepared me for it, not the place but the feeling. 'I have the perfect music for this morning, for this moment.'

Spook looks at me.

* children

I laugh, delighted with myself. 'You'll see.' I take out my phone and scroll through my songs. 'It's one of those "hidden" tracks, kind of appropriate.'

Spook leans over to my phone and snorts. 'Bunch of nancy boys.'

'Listen.' I hold the phone up between us. The piano melody floats up and down, soaring and swooping. The sound of birds on the track echo the gulls in front of us. The notes are weightless, as endless as swells on a calm sea. I close my eyes and am back on the board, water lapping, Spook's firm hold keeping me next to him. The voice is naked but strong. The words are about letting go, taking flight, a love song to freedom. It is as if we invented this bit of paradise, this bit of morning. If only I could bottle this moment and carry it with me everywhere, it could be my protection against Mum and Rory and the rest of my life.

When the notes finish, disappearing into the waves, Spook takes my hand. His eyes search for mine. 'Grace,' he says in a voice that makes my stomach swoop and dive. He lets go of my hand and brushes a clump of salt-heavy hair from my face. 'That's your song, y'know. You have the soul of a bird – you're a searcher.'

I lean into him. The difference in our ages means nothing. I have never felt happier than in this moment. I feel my heart take off and soar high above the endless ocean.

Louisa is on the deck when we arrive back. 'Where have you been?'

'For a surf – sort of,' I reply, glancing at Spook. When I look back at Louisa, I can see her mind working. 'It was very cold,' I add pointlessly.

'I heard you leave,' she says with an ill-disguised accusation in her voice. 'Brett and I are going to the garage to buy more charcoal. Helen and Theresa are coming over later.'

I have to shield my eyes from the sun as I look up at her. 'Cool,' I say lightly. Helen and Theresa love Louisa because she is exotic but similar, but they have no idea what to make of our friendship. I feel severely autistic around them. 'Ask them about themselves,' is Mum's solution to shyness. 'People are dying to talk about themselves, especially men.' But I can never think of the right question to ask.

'Why are you irritated?' I ask her when I get to the deck.

Louisa's arms are crossed. 'You could have left a note.' She lowers her voice. 'We know jack-shit about this guy, Grace.'

No, you can't ruin this, Louisa. Not after the best morning of my life. I take a deep breath. 'I didn't want to wake you. I'm sorry you were worried.'

'He is a complete stranger, Grace, with no fixed address,' Louisa continues, exasperated.

I try to tease her out of it. 'I'm not exactly kidnap material.'

Louisa is about to say something else, but Spook appears at the top of the stairs with both boards. 'Could you grab more beers while you're out?'

Louisa frowns at him. 'It's Sunday – I doubt you'll find anywhere on this entire coast selling alcohol.'

'The Shop and Save on the other side of the location* will. Tell the Chinese manager Wan what you want and he'll take you around the back.'

Louisa lets out a short laugh. 'That's so dodgy.'

---

* township

Spook shrugs and cracks a crooked smile. 'This is the wild, wild West Coast, baby.' He pulls a wallet from his pocket. It's made of beaten-up blue canvas, the sort ten-year-old boys buy in surf shops. 'Drinks are on me today. Get a bottle of tequila too –' He inclines his head towards me – 'for the fresh-airian.'

I look down to hide a smile.

Louisa looks at the wad of notes in Spook's outstretched hand. 'No, really.'

'I insist – it's the least I can do for our future president.'

To my surprise Louisa laughs and takes the cash. 'See you later,' she calls.

I walk inside, trying to figure out Louisa's wild changes in attitude. Yesterday morning she was positively begging Spook to stay; five minutes ago he was an untrustworthy stranger, but now he's OK. Somehow he manages to wrong-foot her at every turn.

The thought of Helen and Theresa's imminent arrival spurs me into going for a run. God forbid they arrive before Louisa returns. The wind has picked up by the time I'm back on the beach. I start at my normal pace but my ankle hurts to the point that I'm forced to adjust it to a fast hobble. The beach is littered with washed-up branches of seaweed. Kelp flies hover above them in little nuclear clouds. A handful of walkers dot the sand in the distance. After this morning I feel as if I have more claim on this coast. It has dug itself into me. Ahead of me three girls in bikinis run across the sand into the water. They jump up and down, screaming at the brain-freezing temperature. I smile. Eventually one of them ducks under a wave. Less than a moment later she emerges shouting. Her friends cheer. Louisa pops into my head. On this endless stretch of white sand, on this coastline that has withstood the most violent storms, with the salt-saturated air like a double espresso running through my veins, I feel that I can fix anything.

By the time I've turned around, the girls are back lying on their towels. A couple comes into view, walking side by side, holding their shoes in a clasp behind their backs. You can tell they are middle-aged by the way they walk. Even though they are surrounded by huge sea and sky, they are both looking down, as though they are having a serious conversation. Or maybe they've seen it so many times they don't notice it any more. The woman is wearing a red costume under beige Bermuda shorts. She stops, bends down and picks something up. She shows it to the man, then pockets it. It makes me look down. Dotted along the sand are mussel shells, but unlike I've ever seen before. These are the perfect shade of blue, as if the sea has gently rubbed them down to reveal their hidden beauty. I can't believe I'd not noticed them. I search until I find two unbroken ones and take them back for Louisa.

There is no sign of Louisa and Brett when I get back. Spook is spread out, fully clothed, on my bed. The only sound is the rattling of the wooden window-frames in the kitchen. I put the shells on Louisa's bedside table, and make a cup of tea. I wander back into my room. Spook's sleep is so deep that he could be dead. I sit down on the bed opposite and watch him. What is it that makes him thirty-five? His skin is more leathery and lined, with little blood capillaries scattered about his nose. His upper arms are thick and strong, that must be the surfing, but his belly is decidedly flabby.

'Are you going to eat me?' he says, his eyes still closed.

I jump back, spilling the tea.

'Now I know how a trapped gecko feels.' His eyes crinkle up at the sides and he starts laughing.

'Isn't the whole point about geckos that they don't get trapped? They drop their tails and run.'

'So that's where I went wrong.'

I want to lie down next to him and rest my head on his upper arm. I've never seen such a solid arm. Mum's arms are yoga-toned and bony. I could happily fall asleep on an arm like Spook's. With a jolt I realise I'm staring at him; he's waiting for me to say something. 'Shower,' I manage at last.

Louisa has dragged mattresses out onto the deck. Helen, Theresa and Louisa are stretched out across them. Brett and Spook are suspiciously absent. I imagine them at the other side of the house, away from the 'oh my gods' and the diet talk. As I step outside I'm convinced that the laughter coming from the mattresses stops abruptly. Helen is a hockey player. Her breasts, which have a life of their own on the hockey field, spill out from her blue bikini.

Theresa, sitting on a separate mattress, has a baggy white T-shirt over her green bikini. It looks fantastic. She looks up. 'Hi, my love.' The 'my love' thing has been going on for about a year. They call everyone from strangers in the street or little Grade Sevens to the school secretaries 'my love'. Instead of saying goodbye, they say 'love you', and 'love you more'. It drives me crazy. Louisa never says it unless they are around.

Helen looks up from the magazine on her lap. 'Oh my god, you look like a supermodel in those shorts.'

Louisa smiles. 'See, I told you – Agyness Deyn from top to toe.'

Theresa frowns. 'Is Agyness Deyn still considered a supermodel?'

Helen thwacks Theresa with the magazine. 'Seriously, Grace, you've got it – see, it's here on the front cover: "*Hollywood goes gaga for the thigh gap*".'

'I don't think it's possible to be a healthy weight and have a thigh gap,' says Theresa, flicking through the magazine.

'Of course it is, my love, it depends on your body type,' replies Helen. 'Unfortunately for me it's not possible to have a thigh gap.' She shrugs. 'It's not in my bone structure.'

'What?' Louisa laughs. I smile. Helen can pull a laugh out of any situation.

'Didn't you know?' Helen continues, wide-eyed. She bats her hand. 'Ag, if you're fit and healthy, who cares?'

'Right on, sister!' says Louisa and high-fives Helen. Her voice is louder, her smile wider since Helen walked up the stairs.

The wind has picked up. Every now and then it delivers a sharp gust, as if making up for its late start.

'Come and sit with us,' says Louisa to me and I realise I've been hovering like a moron while this inane discussion has been carrying on.

'Nah, I'll sit at the table,' I reply, and turn, but not before I catch the look of exasperation on Louisa's face.

Theresa pulls out a plastic tray of carrot muffins.

'I *love* those,' groans Louisa. I look down at the two carrots I've brought outside.

'They're low fat,' says Theresa.

'And if you break them open you release some of the calories,' says Helen.

Louisa laughs. She seems to laugh at everything Helen says today. Why does she turn into a dumbed-down version of herself around Helen and Theresa? I sit at the picnic table, working away at a splinter in the wood. I had a dream once where I was picking at a bulbous lump on my big toenail. The nail peeled off. Underneath it a mucus-covered black beetle was living in my nail bed. I had another one soon after where I was scratching away at a scab on my knee. Under the scab my grandpa's war medals were buried in my skin. Rory would froth with excitement at hearing those dreams.

Brett appears with a pair of speakers and laptop. As he connects them up the music starts with a loud bark. I imagine the released calories hovering in front of the speakers, bumping into each other in fright. Brett lies back on the mattress, resting his head on Louisa's lap. 'Which one of us will be the first to die?' he asks with his mouth full of muffin.

'You're hungover, Brett, not dying,' says Louisa. She licks her fingers. 'But seeing as you ask: Grace will die first.'

'Why do you get to decide?' I ask, which gets a laugh out of Helen.

'You're starving yourself. It's the logical conclusion.' Louisa fixes me with angry eyes. Is this because I won't sit with them? Theresa shoots me a triumphant look.

'You only see things from your point of view.' I wish I hadn't left those shells next to her bed.

'What's the other point of view?'

Helen and Theresa have gone silent; their eyes dart between Louisa and me.

I pause. 'This is a ridiculous conversation.'

A little later Spook emerges. His hair is wet from a shower. He's wearing the same baggy board shorts but a different T-shirt, from the pile on the back seat of his car, I imagine. 'Afternoon, ladies.'

'Hiya, handsome,' replies Brett in a falsetto voice. Spook picks up his surfboard and wanders over to my table.

Helen sits up, thrusting forward those whoopee-cushion breasts. 'We met the other night.'

'We did,' says Spook and winks at her. Theresa's interest has picked up at the sight of Spook. How long will it be before this gets back to my mum?

Spook rests his board over the table next to me. He takes out a battered credit card and starts scraping away at the wax.

Theresa turns to Brett. 'When are you off? Where are you going?'

Brett yawns loudly, and sits up, leaning on his right arm. 'I'm going to surf the seven seas. And Louisa will be waiting for me in our beach hut, wearing a sarong and pansy* shells for a bikini.'

---

* Similar to 'sand dollars', pansy shells are actually flat sea urchins with a delicate five-petal pattern in their centre.

Louisa laughs. 'In your dreams. There are no pansy shells in my plans. My plans feature a big house, a ring and a BMW cabriolet.'

'Sounds fun. Not,' says Brett.

'It's going to be awesome.'

Helen and Theresa laugh. 'Is the BMW a deal-breaker?' asks Helen.

'It is,' says Louisa. I look at her. Since when did social workers drive cabriolets? Only in Louisa's head do the two go hand in hand.

Brett gets up, crosses the deck and leans against the railing. His legs are skinnier than mine. His torso is so lean that it seems vacuum-packed. He picks up Spook's binoculars from the table and scans the bay. Four tankers dot the horizon.

'Another fucking beautiful day,' he says, looking out.

'You mean "Oh God, not another fucking beautiful day",' I say.

'What?'

'That's the quote, from the film *White Mischief*.'

'I'm not quoting.' Brett's confusion makes Spook laugh. He replaces the binoculars on the table.

I pick up one of my carrots. As a snack they are unbeatable. They last for ages. The chatter on the mattresses picks up again.

'What you're doing to that carrot is actually pornographic,' says Spook without looking at me.

I smile. I feel Louisa watching us across the deck. Her comment about me starving myself still stings. She made me sound like a freak. 'Something happened while we were coming back from Lambert's Bay yesterday,' I say to Spook, too softly for Louisa to hear. 'We were almost hijacked.'

Spook stops scraping.

'But actually it felt more like they were chasing us.'

'What kind of a car?'

'It was old and black. Maybe a Golf?'

Spook puts the credit card down. He walks around the table and stops in front of me. 'What happened?'

'It came up right behind us. The driver and passenger were pointing and yelling at us. Then they sped away.' The story sounds silly. 'Louisa didn't want me to tell you, but it's your car.'

Spook chews his lip, hands on his hips.

'Do you know them?' I ask.

'Why do you ask that?' he laughs.

I shrug. 'Louisa thinks it was just some stupid guys but they seemed to recognise your car.'

Brett turns the music up, interrupting Spook's answer. Spook puts the credit card down. He leans backwards and massages the base of his spine. 'This music is *kak**. I need to stretch my legs. Do you want an outing?'

'Sure.' I get up. Louisa stops mid-sentence and looks at us. 'See you in a little bit,' I say. She turns back to the others without commenting.

Baboon Point's streets are narrow; some more like tracks than roads. Chunky slabs of tar give way to gravel and shallow pot-holes in places. Sandy, stubby grass verges act

* rubbish

as pavements; their thirsty tendrils reach out to each other across the road. As we get further away from the mattresses, I feel my mood rise. They will be discussing us of course, but I don't care.

Some of the houses we pass look like heavy Lego blocks, built within a metre of their boundaries. They glare down on their smaller bungalow or clapboard neighbours. Most of them are locked up, waiting for the holiday season to start.

The wind has been gathering ferocity – the 'tender hills' from this morning look dusty and bare. There is no place to hide when the wind blows on this coast.

Spook is barefoot. Now that I think of it, the black boots in the living room have remained mostly unused. 'Don't you wear shoes?'

'Not often,' he replies.

The wide-eyed ocean boy Spook from this morning has withdrawn. I want him back. 'Where do you live?'

'Wherever I need to be.'

'Yes, but where are your things?'

Spook bends down, picks a *duiweltjie** thorn from the sole of his foot and throws it away. 'Bastards,' he mutters. When I'm sure he's not going to answer my question he says: 'Soon after my ma left, my dad took me to the observatory for my birthday. I lay there in one of those reclining dentist chairs, little *laaitie* that I was, looking up at the heavens. I was scared, I started chunking**. My dad had to take me out.'

'Why were you scared?'

_____

*   little devil
** crying

85

'I realised how totally insignificant I was. Parents always tell their kids, "You're my special boy." I understood that day that it's all crap. You're not special. We might as well do what we feel like because there is no reason to anything.'

'Wow. Have you considered a career in motivational speaking?'

Spook laughs. 'But when you accept the randomness of it all, you're free.'

We reach a crossroads. The streets are empty save for the ADT* security guard on his bicycle.

'Do you want to go further?' Spook says, glancing down at my throbbing ankle.

'Sure.' It's exercise.

We walk on, turning right or left in unspoken agreement. 'You know why it's called Baboon Point, right?' Spook says.

'Because of the baboons?'

'No. The silhouette of the rock face at the tip of the point looks exactly like a baboon.'

'So it's literally Baboon Point.'

'That's how they roll on this coast.'

'Do you ever see the baboons around? Everyone seems to make such a big deal out of them.'

'Nah, they're crafty buggers. They wait until they see you drive off before they come and wreak havoc.'

'If it weren't for those ADT guys riding around you could camp out here for months without anyone knowing,' I say.

'Not any more. These days the houses have CCTV.'

* a private security company

I swivel around, trying to spot a camera. 'Where would you go if you wanted to disappear?'

He gives me a sharp look. It takes a moment for his face to soften. 'Karoo maybe. Are you planning on disappearing?'

'I may have to if my mother doesn't leave me alone.'

The word 'poaching' has been spray-painted on the stop sign in front of us. Someone else has crossed it out and sprayed the word 'graffiti' under that.

'Can you believe those poaching syndicates involved Chinese triads and everything?' I say.

Spook grunts.

I'm talking too much but his silence is making me nervous. 'I had no idea someone could exist without a proper job.'

Spook looks at me. 'You mean me? You'll find people do all sorts of jobs you've never heard of.'

We reach the hotel. What few shops there are, are shut. The centre of town is deserted apart from a cluster of kids kicking around a football in the middle of the road. Although some shops close on a Sunday in Cape Town, it's never empty. This is almost creepy. Baboon Point must be one of the few towns left in the world that still shuts down on a Sunday.

Spook walks towards the cash machine. Alongside it, outside the liquor store, a row of men sit along a bench. Apart from the odd comment, they are silent and unmoving. A little further away is a clump of teenagers leaning against the wall. Everyone seems to be watching and waiting, but for what? Someone bumps against me. I turn as a tiny woman, no taller than my shoulder, pushes past me. She is wearing a pair of pink and black leggings and what could be a child's dress. Her head is covered with a grubby *doek** and her face looks a hundred years old. She marches up to one of the men on the bench and starts yelling at him. But he doesn't even look at her, let alone reply. Eventually she turns and walks away.

'Imagine living and working here every day, all year around.' Perhaps it is due to the parched wind that has taken over today, but there is no sense of the wild and untamed coast among the locals. They seem listless, left behind by the rest of the world.

Spook pulls out his wallet. 'Don't be so judgemental. Take the owner of the booze shop. Maybe he is one of the world's greatest philosophers. He levitates when there's no one there.'

I snort. 'He's more likely to spend all day watching sport while he rests his beer on his obese belly.'

'Wow! Don't mess with the hungry chick!'

I turn away as he enters his PIN. The wind makes me feel itchy. Out of the corner of my eye I notice a car pulling away from the stop sign.

'Spook!' I tug at his arm.

'Hmm.' Spook is staring at a mini print-out and tapping the edge of his card against the machine.

'It's that car again.'

'What?'

'The car we saw in town.'

'Are you sure?' Spook's eyes focus.

'I think so. Maybe not.'

---

* a square headscarf

Spook is quiet for a moment. He looks around. 'I need to make a call.'

Spook is leaning against the blue rim of the payphone booth. I watch him from a few metres off. Who is he talking to? He's constantly shifting – from one foot to another; looking down, then up at the sky; fiddling with the green Telkom sign embedded in the metal rim of the booth. Is Louisa wondering where we are? Or is she so immersed in her get-along-gang that she's barely noticed?

In an abrupt movement he replaces the receiver and walks back to me. 'Let's go.'

'I've never used a payphone in my life.'

'There are a lot of things you haven't done,' he replies, looking up and down the road.

I make a face at his back.

A minivan taxi approaches. It is a buttercup yellow, advertising Kellogg's Crunchy Nut. There is a boy leaning out of the window, scanning the quiet roads for potential customers.

'Where are you going?' Spook calls.

'Beach Road,' the boy replies in a bored voice.

'Cool,' says Spook.

The boy opens the sliding door and sits back in the front row seat to let us pass. All the while the driver has not quite come to a stop.

Spook ushers me into the van. The grey plastic-coated seat covering has been patched with green adhesive squares the size of big bottoms. 'What are we doing?' I ask.

'Your ankle's sore,' he replies, as if that answers my question. This is Spook's life, I think, picking up arbitrary taxis going in random directions.

We're the only passengers apart from two big ladies in the back seat who stop talking briefly as we sit down. The window next to me is a cloudy smudge from a previous customer's hair gel. I think about drawing my curly wave pattern on the window but decide against it in case the boy tells me off. The women behind us return to their conversation, still with their eyes on us. Louisa's mum would have a fit if she knew Louisa took taxis with me. But then she has nothing to do all day but cart her children around.

The driver turns and mutters something to the boy. He doesn't respond, but starts counting the change in his money belt.

'Fifty,' he replies to the driver, who grunts in reply.

The boy is about ten years old. He's wearing jeans and a red hoodie and has a cigarette tucked behind his ear. He's chewing gum aggressively.

'Do you go to school?' Spook asks him.

The boy looks up at Spook. He blows a big bubble and pops it. I imagine he's a street kid, a glue sniffer.

'You've got to go to school if you want to end up a rich man,' says Spook.

'Like you?' I say. The boy laughs, which makes me pleased. Spook's tone annoys me. His generation of middle-class white South Africans say '*Eish!*'* and '*Sharp-sharp!*'** They dance to

---

* an expression of commiseration
** used as a greeting or expression of enthusiasm

Freshlyground and are very critical of the lasting legacy of apartheid in their parents' words, but they don't have any real black friends. At least for my generation interracial friendships aren't a project.

One of the women calls out, 'Thank you, driver!' The van stops abruptly and the women get out. The driver speaks on his phone, then turns and says something to the boy. 'We're turning around,' the boy says to Spook.

'We asked for Beach Road, bro,' replies Spook.

The boy shrugs. The driver turns and looks us up and down. I hand the boy eight rand and scuttle out of the van.

'Cheeky shit,' says Spook as the van drives off. 'But it's not far.'

'The beach?' I ask.

'No, the 'Loper.' Spook is indicating a worn sign, which points us in the direction of 'The *Strandloper* Pub'. Underneath someone has added 'warm beer, lousy food'. He looks pleased with himself.

'I haven't heard of it,' I say.

'Like I said, there are lots of things you've not done. We need a beer.'

'A warm beer,' I correct him.

'Want a ride?' he asks.

I nod. My ankle throbs like a silent siren. I hadn't mentioned it while we were walking and I can't help feeling happy that he's noticed. I reach for his shoulders and jump up, instinctively wrapping my legs around his waist.

---

*   Beachcomber. The Strandlopers were a nomadic hunter-gatherer tribe of Khoisan people who lived along the West Coast of Southern Africa.

He folds his arms around them. It's a simple action; necessary to stop me falling off but his arms are like a pair of spark plugs to my nervous system. My shorts barely cover my arse in this position. His arms are wrapped around my whole thigh. I swallow and hold on to my left wrist with my right hand to avoid touching his chest. 'Giddy up,' I say to cover my embarrassment.

'Jesus, you're bony,' he says, 'Relax. Come on, make yourself floppy.'

Short blonde hairs sprout sideways up the nape of his neck. They look bleached against the caramel colour of his skin. I want to sink my lips into the curve, not to kiss it, but to taste such beautiful skin. Then he'd stop, lower me to the ground –

'That's better.' he says.

A couple of cars overtake slowly, making a wide berth around us. How can it feel so normal to be hanging out with someone twice my age? Yet I can't think of anyone I've felt this comfortable with. My mum and her yoga friends are always going on about connected souls.

'Do you believe in reincarnation?' I ask.

He stops and adjusts his grip on me.

'I'm sorry,' I say.

'Your hipbone is hurting me,' he says. 'Reincarnation? No. It's too complicated.'

'Soul mates?'

'Nope.'

'Love?'

'Not really.'

I laugh. 'Redistribution of wealth?'

'Strongly.'

'Assisted suicide?'

'I believe I'm going to dump you on the side of the road if you keep asking me questions.'

I laugh. 'What makes you get up in the morning?'

'Skinny bitches staring at me.'

'Ha ha,' I say. Without thinking I kiss the back of his neck. *What the hell am I doing? This is not me.* Once again I feel out of control. I can feel his body react to the kiss. I blush furiously and bite my lip but after a moment he strokes my leg. It is an awkward movement; it makes me think of kissing boys outside at school discos.

After a couple of blocks he stops. 'Here we are.'

I slide down, too quickly, and land heavily on my ankle.

He takes my hand to steady me. 'Careful,' he says and I laugh. It seems all I can do is laugh and blush. He holds my hand until he realises what he is doing, then lets go.

The Strandloper sits behind a clump of milkwood trees. There are three cars in its gravel car park. 'See that Datsun *bakkie*?' Spook nods his head towards the roughed-up blue pick-up truck in the corner. 'That car has been in that exact spot for three years.'

Suddenly I feel too young and he too old. 'Won't people think it's weird seeing us together?'

Spook laughs. 'Nothing is weird at the 'Loper.'

Wooden stairs, cloaked in the overhanging milkwoods, lead up the side of the building. A barefooted girl about my age is sitting on the bottom step. She turns and looks at us, but seems too stoned to manage to lift her lids all the way. She looks as though she's been sitting there since last night.

'Sisi, you need to sleep,' says Spook as we pass. She giggles.

The entrance to the bar is at the top of the stairs. Through the doors one can vaguely make out a three-sided bar at the back and at the far side of the room a couple of pool tables. A glint of sunshine catches my attention and I follow it onto a large sun-drenched deck. 'Wow!' I breathe. It has the most extraordinary view of the bay. White sand stretches as far as you can see; the late morning sun against the clear sky makes the sea appear dazzlingly blue.

'And you haven't heard of this place?' asks Spook, watching my reaction. He leans slightly into me as he points to a rocky outcrop on the near corner of the beach. 'See that swell a few metres out – that is the best longboard break in Southern Africa.' Spook continues to describe the break. The words mean nothing to me but the rhythm of his voice reminds me of the lapping water this morning. 'Most of the scars on my body are thanks to this coast,' he finishes.

I follow him back past the long wooden tables and benches and a smattering of Sunday drinkers, feeling the fizz where his skin touched mine. *Stop it, Grace!*

Inside the gloom is momentarily blinding. The air has been settled here for a long time. It smells of old men and cheap tobacco.

The bar is lined with rubber beer mats and two enormous ceramic ashtrays.

'When you said institution, I thought you meant in a good way.'

'Ha!' Spook rubs the back of his head. He places his hands on my shoulders. 'Consider this an important day in your education.'

There is the snap of a fridge door and a grunt. A clipboard and pen appear on the counter top, followed by a thickset, balding man. He glances at us, then turns and shouts at the swing doors behind him. 'Sherry!'

The doors part. Sherry is wearing a Lycra leopard-print top stretched over her large breasts. Her brown hair is in a tight perm.

'Yes?' She addresses Spook, yawning at the same time.

Spook takes his time. He looks back at the man, who has resumed his stocktaking. 'Is that your dad?' Spook says in a loud whisper to Sherry.

She laughs.

'Watch it,' the man grumbles from behind an aluminium fridge door.

'Are you old enough to be serving alcohol?' Spook continues.

Another man, old and curling in on himself, shuffles up next to us. Sherry nods at him and reaches for a pint glass. She places it under the Castle Stout tap and pulls the lever, and returns to Spook. 'I'm old enough to be your mother.'

Spook laughs. 'That's OK.'

I move away, pretending to examine the photos that cover the wall next to us. Most of them are of big men with their arms around each other, girls kissing, or Sherry pulling faces. I half expect to see Spook grinning out from one of them. *You're losing it over a guy old enough to be your dad*, I tell myself. *Pull yourself together*.

'Is Marvin around?' I hear Spook say.

I turn. Sherry sniffs and itches her ear. 'Haven't seen him.'

'OK,' Spook replies. 'No probs.' He nudges me with a bottle of Black Label. I look at it dubiously. One beer is the equivalent of three slices of bread, more or less. When last did I eat three slices of bread? I'd rather eat the bread than drink the beer. In my mind's eye the slices become warm, spongy doorstoppers, with a gooey mixture of butter and marmalade dripping off the sides.

'I asked for tequila but she said you looked like trouble,' Spook says. 'Do you want to shoot some pool?'

'It's not really my thing,' I say, trying not to grimace at the sour barley taste.

'Good,' Spook replies and hands me a cue. 'I like winning.'

The man with his pint of stout settles at a nearby table and makes no secret of watching us. I take a shot. 'Ha!'

Spook raises an eyebrow.

'Beginner's luck,' I say.

'Let's hope so.' After his shot, Spook steps back. 'Thank goodness they don't have darts here.'

I laugh. He catches my eye across the table. I bend forward to line up an easy shot.

Spook copies me, as if measuring my chances from his side. He studies my face, which makes my nose itchy. 'Do you look like your old lady?'

'What?' I stand up and rub my nose. 'No. I look like my dad. Apparently.' I lean back to take the shot but the balls jitter in my vision and I miss.

'Fuck,' I straighten up. 'Why do you ask?'

Spook is grinning. 'To put you off.'

'*Boet**!' calls the man from the table. 'Don't you feed your chick?'

We look at each other. 'Only when she's good,' Spook replies, holding my gaze.

The man has a throaty laugh. 'She must be a naughty girl.'

Spook drinks three beers to my one. After two games, both of which he wins, he wanders back to the bar and starts chatting to the manager. Do I join him? He seems to have forgotten me. I study the cue, aware of the old man watching me. I rub chalk on the end. When I look back at Spook, he's settled on a chair. There is nothing for me to do, so I walk outside and sit down at a table. The day has ripened into a perfect heat. The milkwoods shield the deck from the wind but their sweet, almost rotting odour pulls at my stomach. It feels like an emotion. I pick up my phone to take a picture of the view, but all I see in the sunlight is the reflection of my face frowning back at me. *Come outside, Spook, follow me out here*.

A half-empty packet of chips lies open on the table. A seagull lands on the edge of the table and looks at me sideways.

'Shoo.' I flap my hand in its direction. Instead it hops closer, keeping an eye on me. 'Go away!' I reach over, scrumple up the packet and stuff it down the umbrella hole in the middle of the table. 'It's gone, you see! It's finished!' I shout at the seagull and find myself crying.

* Bro

* * *

The week after my mother came in I stood just inside Rory's office. 'You should have told me you were going to get my mum in.'

'Have a seat,' he replied. Instead of sitting down I stared at the books on shelves. Two hundred ways to fix kids.

'That was a betrayal of trust,' I said.

This upset him, I could tell by the startled look on his face. 'I'm sorry you see it that way. I'm trying to –'

'What?'

'Look out for you, help you make the right choices next year.'

'And when did I ask you to do that?' The words were out before I'd thought them.

Rory looked at me. He seemed sad. He swallowed and clasped his hands together. 'Grace, I'm not your friend,' he said quietly. 'I'm a guidance counsellor, that's my job.'

The sun is directly above, pressing down on the top of my head. I close my eyes, tilt my head up towards it. Something brushes my foot. It's the seagull under the table, pecking at the packet of chips.

I was rude. I said something like, 'Don't flatter yourself.' I should have simply walked out. After that he seemed to behave as if someone was watching us. He would conduct our sessions as if he were reading from a script: 'I've talked to lots of girls like you who are struggling with their body image.'

'I'm not struggling with my body image.'

Rory's face suggested that he disagreed. 'What would you say you're struggling with?'

'Nothing,' I snapped. 'This is who I am.'

At the same time the more distant he became, the more I would say things I didn't necessarily mean. One day I walked in with the words: 'My mother is scared of me. I'm her real-time horror film.'

Rory didn't say, 'Now that's not true,' or 'I'm sure she loves you very much.' Instead my words hung about us in the air, the sound of my voice unable to find an exit in the poky office.

'During the day I pile up things to tell her, but when she walks into the room and I see her eyes, it makes me mean. Mute and mean.' The words came out in a rush and just as quickly there was nothing left to say. One day I asked him the one question that had been on the tip of my tongue since I first walked into his poky room. 'So what is wrong with me?'

For a moment the old Rory came back. He looked horrified. 'Grace, there's nothing wrong with you. You're wonderful.' Then he blushed and cleared his throat. 'But you're struggling at the moment with the changes in your life.'

He wouldn't let go of the idea of that stupid centre for teenagers 'who are not coping for whatever reason but are in no ways sad, hopeless weirdos'. 'One visit, please,' he kept asking, 'They have a Thursday afternoon group. I can even drop you off after school.'

The building looked like a large Victorian house on the outside but as soon as you walked in it smelled of instant coffee and paper and hospital cleaner. There were noticeboards in what was once a large entrance hall with Fire Evacuation Procedures and Weekend Emergency Contact Numbers. As soon as Rory left me at the front door, I knew I'd made a mistake. I followed the receptionist up a flight of stairs into a large room. It had a blue carpet and long windows. Slatted office blinds scissored the afternoon sun. The rooms had kept their original decorative cornicing and plasterwork on the ceiling but the central fitting had been removed and replaced with fluorescent tube lights. 'Fuck you, Rory,' I muttered under my breath. In the middle of the room sat eight kids and a staff member in a circle. They all seemed to burrow away from each other into the hospital-issue armchairs. Most of the afternoon passed in silence or mumbled responses to the woman's questions. There was only one other white person there – he looked like he could be a friend of a friend. He answered her questions politely. Towards the end of the session she asked him what he was feeling. He smiled and stared at the floor. We all knew that he didn't want to speak but the social worker kept digging about for something more. Finally he shook his head, then looked up at her. His face had changed – it looked hard and old. His knuckles were white and blotchy red. 'I feel so angry I could kill somebody.' I knew then I could never spend three months in an institution where the truth slipped out so randomly.

Spook appears with two more beers, hands me one and sits down. I sip at it, determined not to think about bread. Or Rory.

Worried that Spook will notice my mood, I start talking. 'My god, these milkwoods smell awful.'

'I don't mind the smell.'

'Oh please.'

'Seriously.' He has a deep sip of beer. 'Do you know about the Post Office Tree in Mossel Bay?'

'I do not,' I reply.

'Way back –'

'When?'

Spook hooks his arm around my neck and rubs the top of my head. 'Stop being so punchy! A very long time ago.' He pauses, furrows his brow and looks up at the sky in mock concentration. 'Five hundred years ago, for argument's sake, Portuguese sailors who had stopped at Mossel Bay tied a shoe to a milkwood tree. In it was a letter saying that Bartholomew Dias had drowned. A year later the guy to whom it was addressed picked it up, out of the shoe.'

'Great historical factoid. Well done.'

Spook laughs, leans his head back and closes his eyes. I pick at the label on the beer bottle, wondering why it is that when Spook's around the thoughts that normally pinch so hard seem to lose their grip. I feel closer to the person I'd like to be.

'Why don't you eat?' he asks.

I sit up in surprise. He hasn't moved. There is no soft concern in his voice, he sounds curious. 'Depends who you ask. Louisa thinks it's attention-seeking. My mum thinks I'm punishing her. Rory has a bullshit theory about delaying womanhood.'

'What do you think?'

No one has ever asked me that question before. They've told me to eat; they've threatened me with hospital and end of friendships and death. I take so long thinking about it that I suspect Spook may be asleep. I hope so. 'It makes me feel sloppy and needy,' I say. 'I know that sounds weird.'

Spook shrugs and yawns. 'Everyone's weird.'

I get the feeling he's studying me. 'What?'

'Nothing.'

'No, really.'

'I haven't met anyone quite like you for a very long time.'

'I find that alarming because I get the feeling you know a fair number of oddballs.'

Spook laughs and strokes the back of my head. 'You're an original, not an oddball.'

Inside the telephone rings. After a moment a man yells, 'Sherreeee!' Sherry yells a muffled reply but the meaning is clear.

'That day my mom left, when I was seven . . .' Spook starts talking, then lapses into silence. I'm confused by this disjointed conversation. Perhaps he smoked something while he was inside?

'From then on it was as if me and my dad kept our ears pricked, waiting for her to open the door, dump her keys, yell at the dog.'

'My dad and I,' I say. His confusion makes me laugh.

After a moment he joins me. 'Right, your turn.'

'What?'

'Tell me something you've never told anyone.'

I focus on the seagull scrounging around under the tables, trying to sort out my thoughts. Is he playing with me? But why would he? Suddenly a desire to talk overwhelms me and the words start spilling out. 'For a long time I used to bug my mum about who my dad was, why she didn't tell him she was pregnant. Lots of kids at school had divorced parents, and just because he and my mum weren't together didn't mean I shouldn't have a dad. Her reason was always the same. "There wasn't enough between us, Gracie. There wasn't enough there; it would never have worked." There wasn't enough for a relationship, but there was enough for a baby. Almost.' I breathe. The words are coming out in a jumble. They sound illogical. 'I think I'm incomplete. There isn't enough of me. You know how foetuses spontaneously abort if there is something wrong with them, I think I was never meant to happen.'

The words, so heavy inside, finally spoken, are weightless. I try to grab them back but they are gone. Spook doesn't say anything. Poor guy, what is there to say? 'That doesn't make any sense, forget it.' I mumble, embarrassed.

'You are complete, Grace.'

'Spare me.'

'There is so much of you to go around. Bucketloads!'

'Please shut up.'

'Great big spoonfuls of Grace, slopping over the side, impossible to contain!' he shouts.

I'm laughing at the odd looks he is getting from the few other customers so much that I don't hear the man approaching or notice that Spook has stopped short and is sitting up. It is only when the man is standing in front of us that I realise that Spook's whole manner has changed.

103

Although the man is standing with his hands in his shorts pockets, the rest of his body seems alert and tight. He is wearing thick-soled hiking boots.

'The old man of the sea!' Spook says. 'Pull up a pew.'

'Aphrodite inside says you're looking for me,' the man says as he sits down opposite us, straddling the bench. His grey hair is pulled back into a ponytail.

'Aphrodite!' laughs Spook. 'That's a good one. What's going on?'

'Same shit, different day,' he says. He jiggles a bunch of keys on the table. He glances at me, nods and says 'Marvin' by way of greeting.

'I'm Grace, Aphrodite's sister,' I say and laugh.

The man looks confused.

Spook frowns at me. 'What?'

It sounded clever in my head. It must be the beer.

'Hey listen, I spoke to Gary,' says Spook.

Marvin is lighting a cigarette as Spook speaks. His hand freezes. He takes the unlit cigarette out of his mouth and looks at Spook. 'And?' He glances pointedly at me.

'Let me buy you a beer,' says Spook and gets up, following the man inside.

When Spook returns he is alone. He sits down next to me, drums out a rhythm on his thighs.

'How is Marvin?' I ask.

'Hmm?' his says. He stands up. 'Ready?'

Ready for what? I'm becoming tired of not knowing what's going on. 'Sure,' I say, but he's already walking towards the stairs. His pace is too quick for me. 'Let's walk along the beach,' he says when he stops for me to catch up. 'Do you want a lift?' He is impatient, as if he'd prefer to leave me behind.

'No.'

Spook takes the stairs two at a time and disappears into the house. I stay on the grass, unable to gather the energy to climb up to the deck. He's going to leave. In fact, he has already left – his body is simply here collecting his stuff.

'Grace?' I hear Louisa calling.

I'm annoyed and confused. What happened to make him want to leave so abruptly? I scan back over the afternoon, trying to find a clue. *Suck it up*, I tell myself, *it was a one night stand that dragged on too long.*

'Grace, your mum phoned.' Louisa is leaning over the railing, looking down at me.

I squint up at her. 'Not now.' I turn towards the beach. The soles of my feet flinch away from the debris of tiny twigs and stones and dried-out succulents that litter the path. Maybe Spook has a girlfriend whom he's been hanging around for and Marvin came to tell him she's back in town. Or perhaps Spook is married and has been skiving off here for a few days while his wife and young children are out of their minds with worry. But Spook went looking for Marvin – he wouldn't do that if he didn't want to be found.

The tide is out. I follow it across the cold sand until I'm ankle-deep, relishing the freezing sting. The queue of tankers has disappeared from the horizon. They've got what they came for and are already on their way. I think back to Spook's description of the train line running down the side of this coast. If each train is three hundred and forty-two wagons long and each wagon carries one hundred tonnes of iron ore, how long will it be before all that ore has been mined? It sounds like a maths problem. But what is never calculated is the impact on what is left behind – the gaping wound in the earth's crust. The train line will lie silent; weeds will soon creep between the tracks. The tankers will have somewhere else to go.

Spook meets me halfway up the path, car keys in hand. 'I've got to get going.'

'Sure. OK.' I offer him a big smile and turn to look down the beach towards the crayfish factory so he doesn't see behind it. An afternoon haze is forming around the point so that I can't quite see the buildings, but I know they're there.

He reaches out and brushes my cheek, forcing me to look back at him. 'Something's come up.'

'Yup,' I nod. Suddenly I think of the swings in the park near our house, how free I'd feel as Mum pushed me. 'Higher!' I'd command. 'But you'll go over the top,' she'd laugh. 'I don't care, I want to go higher!'

Spook smiles at me now, and kisses my nose.

I turn towards the sea. 'Have a nice life!' I call, determined not to watch him drive away. His car starts up. He hoots once and then he is gone.

'You OK?' Louisa is behind me.

I turn around. She is searching my face for a reaction. 'Sure!' To prove it I smile. 'That must be the record for the longest one night stand.'

'The longest, oldest one night stand,' says Louisa. 'Come. Helen and them have gone. We're going to watch a movie.'

I nod and follow her back. As we reach the house Louisa turns back and hugs me, back to her old self. 'We missed you this morning.' I smile and nod and bite back an urge to cry. *Stop it, Grace, he was always going to go.*

Brett is slumped on the sofa, with his feet on the coffee table. He seems to take up more space without Spook here.

'Any more weirdos you'd like to invite around?' he asks.

'I thought you were supposed to be getting drunk,' I reply, sitting down next to him.

'I'm not a machine, Gracie.'

Louisa hovers in front of the sofa with a large bowl of popcorn. It takes me a moment to realise what she wants. I shift up and she plonks herself between us. She passes me the popcorn. 'It's disgusting, there is no butter on it, so you'd better eat some.'

The movie channel is showing *The Usual Suspects*.

'God, this is really old,' says Louisa as she settles herself into the cushions, like a roosting hen.

'Grace likes old,' says Brett with a mouth full of popcorn.

'Hilarious,' I say.

It feels like we're all OK again, sitting on the sofa, talking shit. This is how this week was supposed to be. I'm still holding my handful of popcorn. I put a kernel in my mouth. I swear I can taste butter. But I can sense Louisa watching, so I make myself swallow it.

Five guys shuffle onto the screen in front of a line-up. I remember from the last time I watched this that I had no idea

107

what was going on for most of the movie. Each of them in turn reads a sentence off a card and passes the card along. The middle guy reads it in a completely deranged voice.

'Oh, that's awesome!' laughs Brett. 'He's so cool!'

'He's so you,' sighs Louisa.

When the advert break comes on, Brett mutes the sound. 'Wouldn't it be cooler if they had ancient ads to match the movie?'

'Jeez, it's not that old,' I say.

'Is that what he told you?' Brett says and Louisa laughs. She gets up and lets the wooden roller blind down over the sliding doors, then disappears. A moment later the bathroom door shuts.

Brett and I sit in the golden-brown light, watching the silent TV.

'You liked him,' I say.

'For an ageing hippy.' Brett sits up and looks at me, serious for a change. 'But there was something odd about him.'

I shrug. What was odd about him was how he made me feel. What was seriously odd about him was that he liked me. Or at least I'd thought so. But I'd been wrong about Rory too.

Brett is fiddling with the remote. 'Louisa, it's starting,' he shouts. When she doesn't appear he calls her again.

'Jeez, relax,' I say.

Brett launches himself on me. 'Gimme the keys, you fuckin' cocksucker muthafucka!' he shouts in a crazed voice and bites my shoulder.

'Ow! Get off me!' I shout, laughing.

He sits back and makes a spitting sound. 'Too bony.'

Louisa comes back and they settle back into the movie. I keep returning to the bar. What happened there? It was as if the Spook I knew and liked walked into the bar with Marvin and a new Spook walked back out.

'Grace!' Louisa and Brett are looking at me.

'What?'

'Your old man is in the movie,' says Brett. 'Watch – Redfoot just mentioned a guy called Spook Hollis.'

Two men are facing each other, talking.

'See? They've just mentioned him again. Oh hang on, Keaton "shivved" him,' says Brett. 'Bastard.' He shakes his head. Louisa giggles.

Louisa disappears to refill the popcorn during the next ad break.

Brett looks at me. 'So you're OK?'

'I'm fine! Don't be such a girl, Taylor.'

He laughs. 'You remember how everyone used to ask if we were twins? We could be now with your crazy new haircut.'

'Take a look in the mirror, buddy – you're not half as manly as me.'

Brett laughs.

As the movie resumes Louisa walks up to the TV, without the bowl, and stands in front of it. 'There's something you need to see.'

'Wait till the next break,' replies Brett, gesturing her out of the way.

'No, you need to see it now.'

Brett rolls his eyes. 'Are we watching the movie or not?'

I raise an eyebrow. 'I thought it was too old.'

I chuck a pillow at him. He's about to hurl it back when Louisa yells at us. She puts a navy canvas rucksack down on the coffee table in front of us.

'What?' Brett says.

'This is Spook's bag.' Behind her a man is trying to smash in the windscreen of a moving car. 'He left it in Grace's room.'

'Awesome. Let's watch the movie.' Brett says.

I've never seen the bag before. It certainly wasn't there when I was folding up his clothes. He must have brought it in this morning when I was running on the beach. If he's left it here, it means he'll have to come back. But why didn't he mention it before he left?

'I looked inside.' At the tone of Louisa's voice, Brett turns away from the screen. He sits up. Louisa is staring at the bag, her expression worried. 'There's a whole lot of money inside.'

'What?' Brett and I ask simultaneously.

Despite the noise of the TV, the room feels very quiet. Louisa returns to her seat between us.

The bag is old and scuffed with the flaking remains of an Adidas logo on the side.

Brett leans forward. 'Why did you look inside?'

Louisa shrugs. 'Curiosity.' She leans forward and unzips it.

'Wait!' says Brett. He jumps up and a few seconds later returns with the kitchen gloves. Louisa raises an eyebrow but puts them on. She picks out a threadbare towel that yesterday had been lying on the back seat of Spook's car. Then comes the money. The notes are stacked in piles of brown two hundreds, blue one hundreds and red fifties, bundled together with elastic bands. Some of the notes are new and crisp, others floppy and curled.

After counting a few stacks Louisa says, 'So they're in thousands.' She lines the bundles up along the coffee table. When the last pile is out, she sits back. 'How much?' She looks at Brett.

'Fifty grand.'

'Rubbish!' she laughs. 'It looks like Monopoly money.'

I'm trying hard not to say anything in case I break the fragile calm in the room.

'Fuck me,' says Brett quietly. In the dappled afternoon light his face is blank. 'Do you think it's a joke?' The thought that Spook is going to jump out any moment, laughing at our gullibility, makes us pause.

'Maybe it doesn't belong to Spook,' I say. 'Maybe we're in the middle of some reality show social experiment: "You find fifty grand in your bedroom – what do you do?"'

'And Spook is the show director, which is why he appeared and then disappeared so quickly . . .' adds Louisa.

'Oh my god, I'm going to be famous!' squeals Brett.

We look at each other. 'Nah, says Louisa, 'that shit doesn't really happen.'

'So what do we do?' I ask.

'Throw a massive party,' shouts Brett, throwing his arms open and his head back. When he sees the expression on Louisa's face, he adds, 'And give the rest to charity?'

'Let's finish watching the movie,' says Louisa. Still wearing the kitchen gloves, she picks up the bag.

111

'I like that look,' I say, indicating the yellow gloves.

'Kitchen chic,' she replies and drops the bag on the floor. It lands with a hard thud.

Louisa frowns. She reaches in again and pulls out a grey hoodie. 'It's heavy,' she says and shakes it. A gun falls to the floor.

My breath catches in my throat the way it did this morning in the sea. Ridiculously, all I can think is that it seems too small to be a real gun. The handle is worn and scratched. The rectangular barrel is smooth, slightly darker than the handle and shiny.

'That doesn't look like a joke,' says Bret.

The rumble of an approaching train grows. It feels oddly comforting to hear it – we may be knee-deep in cash and staring at a gun but the train is still running. Against the screeching steel I ask: 'Is it a revolver?'

'It's a pistol,' replies Brett. His voice has a weird calm to it. 'Don't touch it,' he says as Louisa bends towards it. 'It could be loaded.'

The train noises die away, leaving us in uncomfortable silence. Brett stands up. He walks towards the kitchen, then turns back: 'Fifty grand in a bag? Weird. But fifty grand and a *gun*?' He shakes his head. 'Dodgy. Definitely dodgy. This is your fault,' he adds, pointing at me. 'You brought him here!'

'What?'

'When Spook realises he's left the bag behind, he'll come and get it,' says Louisa, attempting to adopt a rational voice.

But why would he leave it here? I have a horrible feeling about this. 'What kind of person has a *gun*?' I say, thinking aloud.

'My dad has a gun at home.' Louisa shrugs.

'Seriously?' I turn to her, momentarily distracted. I've slept in that house almost every weekend for the past three years without knowing there was a gun in the house.

'Come on, Grace, this is South Africa. He'd never use it, of course.'

That seems counterintuitive – why own a gun if you're not going to use it? Guns belong with drugs and burglaries and random murder. Why would Spook need a gun? And why would he leave it here?

'What do you know about this?' Louisa turns to me.

'Nothing!'

'What did he say on the beach?'

I blink, forcing my mind back. The beach seems a very long time ago. 'He said he had to go.'

Louisa has her hands on her hips. 'And before, what happened when you went out?'

'We walked to the town centre, then to a bar and had some beers. Then we came home. Why is this my fault? You found the bag.'

'Hmf,' she responds and turns back to the bag. Why don't I mention the phone call and the black car, or the dramatic change in Spook after he spoke to Marvin? Why don't I mention that the bag is not something he forgot to take with him, that it's the first time I've seen it, therefore he must have left it behind on purpose?

'We could toss the gun into the sea, take the cash and split. He'd never find us,' says Brett.

'That is the dumbest idea I've ever heard,' I say. 'We should take it to the police station.'

'*That* is the dumbest idea,' says Louisa. 'We are not going anywhere near the police. If this got back to my parents I'd never be allowed to leave my house again. Phone him and tell him to come and pick it up.'

I look at her. 'I don't have his number.' How strange that I know his mum's name and all about his dad but I don't know his phone number.

Louisa thinks for a while. 'We'll leave the bag on the deck and go out, and hopefully it will be gone by the time we get back.'

As we're getting ready to go I walk into the living room to find Brett, wearing the kitchen gloves and holding the gun. He's facing the sliding door so that he can see his reflection. His arms are outstretched at shoulder height; he's holding it with both hands, posing like Jason Statham in an action movie. He grins sheepishly when he sees me. 'Oh come on, everyone wants to know what that feels like.'

'Put it down,' I say, with a feeling of dread. 'Don't you read the news?'

The bag looks odd sitting on the mat outside the sliding door. We argue about how to place it so that it can't be seen from below but is obvious enough that Spook won't bash down the door when he comes back to get it. In the past few hours Spook has gone from being an ageing hippy to a violent outlaw.

Baboon Point is not exactly bursting with options of places to go on a Sunday evening. We take the road that runs behind the crayfish factory. As we round the point I look up. 'Hey, wait! Stop!' I roll down the window and lean out.

Louisa looks around, her eyes big. 'What?'

'Look up at the rocks. Can you see a baboon's face?'

'Grace!'

'Seriously, can you see the shape of a baboon's head in the rock?'

Louisa looks up. 'I guess. Why?'

I settle back into the seat. 'No reason. Just interesting.' I shrug.

Louisa and Brett share a look.

Flat rocks, pummelled smooth by centuries of lashing waves, fan out around the point. It would be a perfect place to watch the sun ripen and spill out over the sea. But this evening it seems half the town has brought out their fishing rods so instead we head for a cave Helen had told us about.

It's a short walk up the side of the hill to the shallow overhang of rocks. The view spans the gentle curve of the white coastline. San handprints cover the rock face at the rear of the cave. The small ochre shapes look more Aboriginal in design than the rock paintings I've seen before. I place my hand against one, trying to conjure up the artist.

'You whites love to connect with your African-ness,' comments Louisa behind me.

'Rubbish,' I say and blush at her perceptiveness.

Louisa chucks a packet of chips at Brett. 'Seeing as Spook's left us with his shit it's only fair we drink his booze,' she says and takes out the bottle of tequila he requested this morning. She sets about making tequila sunrises. Because Louisa always does things properly, along with the orange juice she's brought along a teaspoon and some Grenadine.

'To Spook,' says Brett, raising his glass. 'So long and thanks for the gun, I mean tequila.'

'I wonder where each of us will be this time next year?' says Louisa, looking out over the sea.

'If we took advantage of Spook's little trust fund, we could all be on a beach in Mexico. What did he call it – "the university of life",' replies Brett.

It occurs to me how much I hate those two words 'next year'. If Mum is serious about me not going to university, then I have literally nothing to look forward to. Will the three of us still be having sundowners together a year from now? Will I still know every single piece of clothing in Louisa's cupboard? Or will we look back at this evening as one of the last we spent together?

Voices and car radios float up from the rocks below. 'I thought fishing was a quiet activity.'

Brett bursts out laughing. 'You don't fish at night, you idiot. Hey, if you had to take all the money, what would you do with it?'

'Fifty thousand? I don't know.' I shrug, feeling the familiar panic at not having a plan: *There's no fucking plan.*

Brett laughs. 'I'd turn to my dad and say, "Fuck you, Old Man, you can keep your money, I'll pay for my own overseas trip." He'd never get to hold money over me again.'

'Ooh, fighting talk!' teases Louisa. 'Would you pay him back for that shiny new car he bought you?'

Brett snorts. 'It's a red Ford Fiesta, Lou. He can keep the car.'

Louisa takes a pensive sip of her drink. 'Apart from a massive shopping trip, I'd invest the money.'

Brett and I burst out laughing. 'You're not even eighteen years old and you want to *invest* it?'

Louisa looks at us pityingly. 'Don't come asking me for money one day.'

'I know what I'd do,' I say, 'I'd use it to get as far away from my mother as possible.' I can see it: a beach hut in Indonesia, waking up every day with Spook.

Brett finishes his drink in a gulp. 'Seriously though, please shoot me if I'm like Spook when I'm thirty-five.'

'I'll shoot you before if you like,' says Louisa, 'after all, we have a gun.' She can't help but flash me a look.

'The thing is, he doesn't strike me as a criminal,' Brett continues. 'More a saddo.'

'I thought you loved his "eat, sleep, surf, repeat" lifestyle,' I say.

Brett gives me a withering look. 'Sure, as long as it's based in my Bantry Bay seafront house.'

I wonder if Spook's back at the house now, picking up the bag; whether there is any part of him that is disappointed I'm not there. 'His mum left when he was seven,' I say. They look at me. As soon as I say the words, it feels as if a precious piece of Spook is now worthless. 'Not that that explains the bag,' I add.

Brett laughs but Louisa looks at me for a long time.

The tequila is finished. The sun has slipped behind the horizon. 'Does anyone else feel very un-drunk?' asks Brett as we make our way back to the car. The rapidly darkening sky makes it tricky. I trip over a rock.

117

'Obviously not Grace,' says Brett.

I giggle. 'I can't see.'

Back in the car Louisa finds a message from Helen. 'No parties tonight, they're going to watch a movie.'

'Movie-shmoovie,' says Brett. We all know that we can't go home. The only other option tonight is the hotel.

We are the youngest people there by fifty years. 'OK,' says Brett slowly, looking around as we walk in. Louisa giggles. Shiny fake mahogany panels cover the walls. All three occupants of the bar turn and look at us as we arrive.

We choose a table under the mounted heads of two wildebeest. 'Tonight we drink brandy and Coke,' announces Brett.

'Why?' asks Louisa.

'To fit in,' replies Brett, in a stage whisper. 'Trust me.'

'Drinks are on me tonight,' I say quickly. I don't trust Louisa to order Coke Zero.

Sitting at the bar are two men, watching rugby replays on the TV above the bar. Both of them have their folded arms resting on the counter and a half-drunk beer in front of them. The one closest to me has white hair and a thick moustache. By the time I go back for the second round the rugby has ended and I'm feeling chatty. The man with the white hair is the local superintendent.

'Is there lots of crime around here?' I ask, picturing the bag sitting on the deck.

He shakes his head. 'Nothing. Very little,' he says with a thick Afrikaans accent. 'There was a spate of trouble a few years back, outsiders committing break-ins and petty theft.

118

But they soon found that here in Baboon Point we have zero tolerance for that.' He sips thoughtfully at his beer. 'Now we're left with the usual weekend domestic stuff. And removing boomslangs from properties.' He sits back and rests his arm on his stomach as if he were pregnant. 'Nothing happens here that I don't know about. That's the beauty of a small town.'

I nod and return with the drinks to our table.

'Seriously, Grace, is this age thing becoming a fetish?' says Louisa, her laugh verging on the hysterical.

'That's Superintendent Visser.'

Louisa splutters into her drink. 'One side of the law to the other,' she says too loudly. The alcohol has slowed her reactions. I watch as her face suddenly contracts. 'You didn't mention –'

'No!'

The bag is where we left it. A sharp chill has developed in the air. The brandy and Coke is swilling around my stomach, curdling with the orange juice. I feel like a whale. Perhaps I should make myself sick.

Louisa steps over the bag. She sighs like a disappointed parent. 'Leave it, it will be gone in the morning.'

I feel his hot, snuffly, sleep-heavy breath on the back of my neck. Lying very still, I close my eyes and open them again, just to be sure. A soft breeze from the open window blows life into the air. The night is a perfect warmth.

'Spook?'

'Mmm?

'Why did you go away?'

'I'm right here.'

His body is so close to mine that he feels more like a protective outer shell than a separate person.

I turn over. We are like two limpets clinging together. The moon is waning but there is enough of it to throw a shimmering light on him. His nose is inches from mine. I rub his stubble with the tip of my finger. It reminds me of a cat's rough tongue.

His eyes are closed. I picture him hovering, rocking gently back and forth between sleep and wakefulness. *Don't wake him*, I tell myself, *see if you can catch one of his dreams and ride it with him*. I imagine the two of us standing on his longboard, perfectly balanced.

His resting face is so soft, his gently parted lips are so innocent that I imagine myself as his mother, Cornelia Roux, watching him sleep.

He stirs. His hands find my face, his eyes still closed. 'Gracie.'

'Let me stay with you, Spook. Please. We can live in a cottage next to the sea; you can surf all day.'

'I can't look after you.'

'I don't need looking after!'

Morning is approaching; I need to get through to him. 'Wake up!' I whisper, 'Look at me.'

'Shhhh,' he replies. 'Sleep now.'

'No! We met each other for a reason, Spook. I'm your original, remember? This was meant to be.' But my words are lost in a breaking wave. We are swimming. The water is warm enough to be a bath. He's lying on his back, his toes peeking out of the water. I close my eyes for a moment, and when I look back at him, he's gone. Suddenly, hands around my tummy pull me down, through layers of increasing cold.

When I surface, spluttering, laughing, I hook my arms around his neck. He kisses drops of water off my nose. 'You're the only person in the world who gets me, Spook, you're the only one I feel free with.'

'You are free.'

MONDAY

It feels very early when I open my eyes. The smell of the sea is intense and heavy; it has settled itself in the room. I am alone, in my single bed.

The clouds are so low and dense that I can't see the next-door houses, let alone the beach. From inside it looks as though we have been wrapped up in huge wads of cotton wool.

I pull on a sweatshirt and walk through the silent house, looking for signs of Spook. I can smell him, I can feel his stubble on the tip of the second finger of my left hand. As I reach the locked sliding door and see the rucksack still outside, I have to reach my hand out to the glass to steady myself. No. I spoke to him, I felt his breath on me. I step outside and walk across the deck. Thick wisps of mist swirl about me, through me. I shiver and wrap my arms around myself. If it was a dream, how come it feels more true than anything else in my life? Am I going mad?

I knock on Louisa's door. 'No nakedness please,' I say loudly as I push open their door. They are curled up together. I cannot shake the feeling of Spook. It's not in my head; it's a physical sensation. Then I remember that amputees feel pain in their severed limbs.

I balance my tray of tea and brownies at the bottom of their bed.

'I feel ill,' groans Louisa. She gets out of bed and fishes around in her washbag for a box of Myprodol. Brett turns on his side and pulls the pillow over his head.

'It's still there,' I say, watching her swallow a couple of pills in a gulp of tea. Louisa looks at me, drains her mug and pours another. She gets back into bed. After I've moved the tray, I climb under the duvet at the bottom of the bed. Louisa chucks me a pillow. Once I'm settled, lying top to toe with her, I lie back and close my eyes. What if Spook never comes back? Do we leave the bag here?

'The other night when we were talking about next year – why didn't you tell Spook you were going to study Psychology?' Louisa asks. I steal a glance at her. She is lying back on the pillow with her eyes closed.

'Because according to my mother I'm not going to any more.'

Louisa sits up. 'What?'

'Yup. She's signed me up for some retarded outpatients' group instead where I'll probably have my neck slit by some drugged-up gangster kids. Apparently it's for my benefit.' I used to worry so much about Mum dying that I'd spend hours imagining it: the car accident, the phone call, being left all alone in the world. I'd lie on my bed with tears streaming down my face as I pictured the funeral and me walking all alone behind the coffin. I knew it was weird but I couldn't make myself stop. That Mum disappeared a long time ago.

'It might end up being a good thing,' says Louisa, careful not to catch my eye. I notice that she doesn't say that Mum's ridiculous or that of course she's simply making idle threats.

A 'good thing' would be to wake up every morning in that house by the sea, watching Spook sleep. In winter we could sit in front of a fire while the wind howled around our little cottage.

The sound of a car makes us both sit up. I strain my ears, hoping to hear the clatter of Spook's silencer. Louisa peeks out the bedroom window. 'It's Helen!'

I rush outside for the bag and dump it under the bed.

A few moments later Helen appears. 'Morning, my loves!' She is wearing jeans, a beanie with a pom-pom and her Ugg boots. How much clothing did she bring? I watch her taking in the scene – the three of us lazing in bed, no sign of Spook. She steps backwards and looks up the corridor. Louisa catches my eye.

'Where's your guy?' Helen asks me as she steps into the bedroom.

The mention of Spook brings back my aching for the dream. I rub the tip of my second finger with my thumb. 'He left yesterday.'

'We're going to stock up at the Woolies in Vredendal.' Helen turns to Louisa, 'Do you want to come?'

'Nah,' Louisa says.

I study the duvet cover. It's obvious that Helen wants to stay. I think of the bag and the gun under the bed and start to giggle.

Helen frowns. 'Are you guys stoned?'

'No,' says Louisa, giggling too. 'Call me when you're done shopping.'

As the morning progresses it becomes apparent that we can't have a conversation without mentioning 'the bag'. It's no longer exciting; it has become a reason for us to snap at each other. Each time a car passes I look up, and every time I look up I catch Louisa watching me.

Brett has barely said a word since he got up. His face has a green tinge as he lies on the sofa, flipping through TV channels. Each time one of us talks, he turns the volume up.

I offer to stay at home while they go out. This annoys Louisa. 'You can't babysit a gun, Grace.'

'Fine,' I say. 'We'll leave it here and all go out.'

'Where are we going to go?' snaps Louisa. The mist has not shifted, it is tightly wrapped around the house. Eventually we settle on a walk. With the bag. That way Helen won't stumble upon it if she drops by. Spook will have to wait if he turns up while we are gone.

Stepping onto the beach is like walking into a tunnel of white. Halfway across the sand Brett stops. 'I'm too ill to walk.' He pulls his red hoodie over his face and collapses on the sand.

'Will you keep this?' I hold out the bag.

Brett laughs at the suggestion. 'Just so we're clear, that bag has nothing to do with me. If my dad ever hears about this, he'd cancel my overseas trip.'

'No he wouldn't,' Louisa scoffs.

'He would. He's dying to find a reason not to fork out all that money.'

Louisa crouches down to kiss him and says something that makes him laugh. I turn away, feeling lonely. Rory used to say no one can make you feel anything you don't want to. That's another thing he was wrong about.

Louisa and I walk along the edge of the water, dodging the waves that creep too far up the sand. The mist is so disorientating that I can't work out whether the tide is coming in or going out. We pass a perfect blue mussel shell next to a branch of kelp. Louisa hasn't said anything about the two I left on her bedside table. Every so often a walker looms through the mist, then disappears again. The weight of the bag on my back feels as though I'm pulling Spook along with us. I shift the contents around until the gun is not jabbing against my coccyx.

'Mrs Cele hasn't called since we arrived,' says Louisa, referring to her mother.

'Lucky you.'

Louisa raises a disparaging eyebrow. 'You know my mum. She phones me to tell me she's put the dishwasher on. This kind of silence means trouble. And the only trouble she wouldn't want to tell me about is to do with me. I'm guessing I've been accepted onto the Social Work course.'

'Why is that trouble?'

'I didn't tell her I applied.' Louisa smiles at the look of disbelief on my face. I was surprised when Louisa announced at the beginning of this year that she'd changed her course from a business degree to Social Work, but I didn't think much more than that. How had I missed it?

She puts on her mum's accent: '"Your father does not leave for work at six-thirty every morning so that his daughter will end up a social worker. *Do you take your parents for idiots?* You will get a proper job and make your father proud." Of course, Dad's not the one who objects.'

I'm struggling to stop myself from feeling hurt that she hadn't told me about it. Her application went in months ago. Did she tell Helen at the time? 'Social work is a proper job,' I reply eventually.

Louisa shakes her head. 'According to my mum I won't make any money, no one will want to marry me and dealing with people in need is depressing and thankless.'

'But your mum was raised by nuns,' I say.

'Exactly. Her reason for living is to give her children a different life to hers. She is going to be apoplectic when she finds out, especially as Dad signed the forms without her knowing.'

'Wow.' I almost feel sorry for Mrs Cele. Louisa is so obviously her favourite child, this kind of defiance would be devastating. 'Are you going to stick to your guns?'

'Dunno,' says Louisa quietly. 'So when does your programme thingy start?

'I don't want to talk about it, Lou.' I realise too late that this walk was a very bad idea. To be stuck in a one-on-one with Louisa could end up being disastrous.

'I can't believe you're not going to be starting varsity next year!' That is the sort of thing Theresa would say.

'We were never going to be on the same campus.'

'Still –'

'You won't even notice I'm not there with Helen and Theresa around.'

Louisa stops short. 'What is your problem with them?'

'Nothing! It was a joke.'

We've reached the end of the beach, the crayfish factory looms above. A long row of glassless square windows gapes at the ocean. 'You could just imagine a bunch of corpses in there,' says Louisa, shuddering.

'And a den where a serial killer has covered the walls in photographs and painted over them in blood,' I add.

'Stop it!' says Louisa.

I laugh. I'm about to carry on when something brushes against the back of my legs. 'Jesus Christ!' I shout and whirl around. A bedraggled sheepdog is wagging its tail. '*Voetsek!*'* I shout. I stamp my foot at it.

Louisa throws back her head and laughs. 'Did you think it was the serial killer?' The dog jumps up at her, but she bats it away. She's not a pet person. There is a high-pitched whistle behind us and the dog charges off.

'This mist is freaky. Anyone could be following us.'

'Who would want to follow us?'

---

* Get lost!

'The gangsters, from that car in Lambert's Bay,' I say before I can stop myself.

Louisa takes my arm. 'No one was chasing us, Grace. It was some random car.'

'So you're saying the black car and the bag and Spook disappearing have nothing to do with each other?' Even as I'm speaking the words I know it sounds a little far-fetched.

Louisa gapes at me. 'Is that what you think?'

'No,' I say, looking away.

'Do you want Spook to come back?'

'Well, he has to, doesn't he?'

'That wasn't what I asked.'

As we walk back I can feel the pressure in the air changing. The sun far above is creating a sharp yellowy light.

'Did Mr Thomas suggest the programme?'

'Why are you so obsessed with Rory?'

Louisa stops abruptly. It's because I used Rory's first name. *Dammit.* 'You never talk about him,' she says in a carefully casual voice.

I carry on walking a few paces then turn around and face her. 'There's nothing to say.' *And it's none of your bloody business*, I almost add. 'But you're right, I never talk about him. So how do you know about him?"

She holds up her hands. 'Forget it, Grace.'

She's holding something back. 'Do you discuss me with Helen and Theresa?'

Louisa pulls a face. 'No.'

'Because that will go straight back to my mother and –'

'Grace!' Louisa shouts at me. 'Who do you think told him where to find you that day?'

I look at her, reeling. 'He was taking a walk.'

Louisa sighs. 'Sure, and Father Christmas is real.' She walks past me at an angry pace. Brett comes into view, lying exactly as we left him.

'Are you saying you told him? How did you know where I was?' I shout after her, but she has broken into a run. By the time I reach them she's lying next to him with her head on his chest. I leave them there and head for the path to the house. I round the first corner, brushing a pin-cushion bush out of the way. It's not fair. Less than twenty-four hours ago Spook was simply the oddball stranger with no plans for the rest of his life. This time yesterday we were at the bar. He hadn't yet spoken to Marvin. I feel his arms wrapped around my legs again; the smell of soap on his neck.

The glimpse of a car through the trees makes me stop. It's moving slowly, as if about to turn – is it Spook? Has he come back? It disappears for a moment. I try and stop the smile from spreading across my face. Be cool, Grace! He's only here for the bag. But I don't care. I'm glad the others aren't with me. I'm almost running as I round the curve and come into full view of the house and the drive.

Shit. I sink to the ground. I have to get to Louisa and Brett, I have to stop them making a noise. I scramble back along the path. Louisa is alone. I lunge at her and pull her down. 'What?' she says, too loudly so that I scrunch up my face and shake my head.

'Car,' I breathe.

'What car?' Louisa tries to get up but I pull her back down. 'The black car.'

I follow Louisa, bent double, the bag banging awkwardly on my back, silently begging the dense growth of fynbos* on either side of us to hide our scramble back down the sandy path.

'Brett, get down!' hisses Louisa as he comes into view.

'What?' Brett's surprise wipes away his grumpy expression.

'Get down!' Louisa yanks him by the arm.

'I knew it!' I whisper. We're crouched around the scuffed bag. 'I told you, Louisa! They must have been following Spook.' I feel triumphant, vindicated.

Louisa glances sharply at me then turns to Brett. By the look on Brett's face it's obvious she hadn't mentioned the black Golf following us in Lambert's Bay. As she whispers a hurried, edited version, Brett stands up. 'Brett!' we hiss and pull him down. The heavy mist is evaporating in front of us.

'They're climbing up to the deck,' he says.

'Go and get rid of them, Brett.'

'Why me?'

'They don't know you.' Louisa's whisper is rising.

'This has got nothing –'

Louisa pinches his thigh.

'OW!' He rubs his leg.

'Go,' repeats Louisa, 'before they break the door.'

Brett swears and gets up.

'Don't look back,' Louisa says fiercely.

* Indigenous dense mix of shrub bush

132

He walks forward, his grasshopper legs extending angularly from his yellow and white boardies, making him look no older than twelve.

'Jesus, I hope this works,' whispers Louisa.

'I *told* you –'

'Shush,' Louisa interrupts.

A voice reaches us: 'Hoesit my bru.' It sounds like a bad caricature of a Cape Flats accent.

Brett's response is muffled.

'Nice place, nuh,' continues the oil-on-water voice.

I glance at Louisa. She is frowning in concentration as she listens, hugging her knees. I pick up a twig and run my fingertips along the jagged stem.

'Happy days,' comes a different voice. Of course – there were two in the car. '*Bietjie** *fres* fish and calamari.'

'Can I help you?' says Brett.

'Just a courtesy call,' says the first voice. The other voice laughs. 'We're looking for a friend. Haven't seen him for a long time, so we're trying to get back in touch, see.'

'Are you going from house to house?' asks Brett. I catch Louisa's eye. She shakes her head.

The first voice laughs. '*Lekker*** funny, nuh? No. A friend of a friend said he was staying here.'

'You've got lots of friends,' says Brett.

'Stop being smart, Brett,' whispers Louisa, rubbing her hand over her head. Her hair is shorter than Spook's. Her head has a more graceful curve.

---

*   A little
** Nice [and]

'But I'm afraid your friend isn't here,' Brett continues. 'Never has been.'

'That is odd,' says the first voice slowly. 'Sorry to bother you then.' There is a pause. Louisa and I look at each other, waiting.

'You don't mind if we come inside, nuh.' The politeness of the request is distinctly mocking. 'Leave our number in case he turns up.'

Louisa holds up the house keys. I squeeze my eyes shut.

'No,' says Brett, loudly. 'I mean *yes*, I do mind.'

We're straining to hear their reply but the noise of the approaching train drowns their voices. 'Oh my god, this is not happening,' whispers Louisa.

The steady mechanical hiss and rumble lasts for so long that it seems as if someone has pressed pause on the moment. I picture the three hundred and forty-two wagons, each creaking under the weight of one hundred tonnes of iron ore, and will them to go faster. Louisa looks down at the bag. 'It's not fair to leave Brett on his own.' Her voice is wobbly. 'I'm going to join him.'

'No!' I grab onto her arm. 'They saw us in Spook's car. It will make it obvious that Brett is lying.'

'I don't care!' She yanks her arm free and straightens up.

But a moment later she is next to me again. 'Helen's just driven up!'

I put my hand over my mouth.

'Howzit Brett!' comes Helen's voice. It has an edge to it that's really saying 'who the crap are these people?'.

'Can I help you?' she says, in a voice her mother would use

to talk to the gardener. Only Helen wouldn't realise the danger she's in. 'What? What chap?'

The response is muffled.

'Don't be ridiculous. I'm sorry but if you don't leave I'm going to have to call the police.' Helen's voice is getting louder.

After what feels an excruciating delay the car starts up and reverses. Louisa and I look at each other. I've been sitting on my haunches. My knees are aching; I lean backwards until my bum hits the ground.

I look at Louisa. 'Do you –'

'Shh!' she says and we wait a few more minutes.

'Helen can't know about the bag,' I whisper.

'Leave it here. We'll pick it up when she's gone.'

'You're right, Louisa. We should have gone to Plett,' Helen calls from the deck as we approach. 'You've just missed some seriously skanky guys snooping around. Looking for your guy, apparently,' she adds, looking at me.

'He was never my guy,' I say as we reach the top of the steps.

Louisa steps around me and hugs Helen. 'It's good to see you. It's always good to see you, but right now, particularly so.'

Helen steps back and looks at her suspiciously. 'What's going on?'

Louisa laughs, much higher than her normal gravelly chortle. She looks at me.

Helen turns to study Brett and me. 'You were acting weird

this morning too. I know,' she says slowly, 'you've got hold of some mushrooms, haven't you?'

This starts Brett and me giggling too.

Helen knows she's missing something. Her hands are on her hips. 'Vredendal is crappy,' she says eventually.

Louisa sighs out the last of her laughter. 'Of course it's crappy, but you knew that before you went. Hey – the sun has come out.'

I look up. The sky has transformed into an innocent blue; the solid morning mist belongs to a different place and time.

'We're having a party tonight. You guys have to come. But no more weirdos,' says Helen, looking at me.

'Why don't you hang around for a coffee?' Louisa asks.

'I have to go. The others are waiting for me.'

'The others?'

'We met some guys at that restaurant on the beach. They're coming over.'

'OK,' says Louisa, not quite managing to hide the disappointment. I watch her watching Helen walking back to her car, looking wistful.

'Bye, my love!' I shout after Helen. She turns around and waves.

Louisa glares at me.

A thud makes me jump. Brett has hurled an empty beer can across the deck. It clatters about for a few moments. He stalks after it. Louisa looks at me. The temporary distraction Helen brought has evaporated in the growing heat of the sun.

'Fuck!' Brett shouts at the sea. He turns back to us. 'I am NEVER doing that again.' He's shaking. I think it must be fear but then he looks at me, his face tight with anger and for the first time I see his father in his face. It moves differently. Are our grown-up faces there all along, waiting for childhood to be rubbed away like a scratchcard?

'Get rid of that fucking bag.'

'Brett, chill!' says Louisa.

He turns to her. 'You didn't have to talk to them! They were gangsters, Louisa.

'Two days ago you two are followed by some random car in Lambert's Bay. Now they turn up here, looking for Spook. How the fuck does that work?'

Louisa turns to me.

'I don't know! Will the two of you stop making this out to be my fault – you were the one who wanted to take the car, Louisa.'

Louisa gapes at the words. 'Excuse me?'

'It's true. If you hadn't insisted on taking Spook's car this would not be happening.'

Brett swears again and disappears inside. He returns with his wallet. 'None of this is my fault. Fix it,' he says and disappears down the stairs.

Louisa turns to me. 'But how would they link the car and Spook to this house? They must have been following us. What happened yesterday when you went out?'

'Nothing! I told you! I'm going to get the bag.'

I feel sick as I walk back down the path. Is it time to tell Louisa about seeing the car again yesterday? But I've already denied knowing anything – if I changed my story now, she'd blame all of this on me.

She is in the kitchen when I return. I drop the bag next to the fridge. The heavy clunk of the gun on the floor makes me wince.

She hands me my phone, showing another three missed calls from my mother. 'Get over yourself and call her. Soon she's going to drive up here and that is the last thing we need.'

The impatience in her voice makes me defensive. 'She won't.' I almost wish she would. Those men and the problem of the bag would be no match for my mother in a fury. I turn and open the fridge for the jug of water. I feel Louisa's angry silence. I slowly fill a glass and place the jug on the counter. The cold water slices a path down to my stomach.

The house owner has stuck laminated notices to the fridge.

'Water is a precious resource! Use sparingly!'

'Don't forget to lock away the outside rubbish! The baboons are watching!'

I lean against them, irritated by the number of exclamation marks.

Louisa has picked up her mother's biscuit tin and is tracing the large faded pattern of heavy rose blossoms. It is as familiar to me as Louisa. Each time we walked into her kitchen the first thing we'd do was look in that tin. It was never empty. She opens it now and picks out one of her mother's brownies. 'My mum says she feels sorry for yours. She doesn't know what she'd do if I stopped eating.' She takes a bite of the brownie.

I swallow back my annoyance. 'I haven't stopped eating.'

Louisa rolls her eyes. 'It must be tough on her, dealing with it on her own.'

These comments are straight out of Mrs Cele's mouth. She is always bemoaning the lot of my mother. 'I don't know what I'd do if I were a single parent. It must be so lonely.' Or 'Your mum works so hard, Grace, you must be a good daughter to her.'

What Louisa really means is that she feels sorry for my mother dealing with me. This conversation needs to end. I'm leaving the kitchen as she says, 'Why did you go and see Mr Thomas every week? And then what happened?'

I look down at the floor. The painted white boards could do with another coat. 'Nothing.'

'So why did you stop seeing him?'

I sigh and look up at the ceiling. The white-painted cross-beam has a nail banged into one side. Do the owners hang Christmas decorations from it? 'He felt that I didn't need to see him any more,' I reply eventually.

'Are you joking? Do you know how much weight you've lost in the last three months?'

Of course I do, you idiot! I want to shout. But I look her straight in the eye. 'None, actually.'

Louisa laughs in my face. 'You don't talk, Grace. Not to me, not to your mother. You just keep getting thinner. Who knows what's going on? Do you?'

The doorframe is painted blue-grey. Mum's friend Sophie has a front door painted the same colour. My fingernails have turned purple from gripping onto it.

Louisa takes a breath and turns to me. 'I think you created a set of parents out of Rory and your mother. Something happened and now you're grieving for him.'

I laugh. 'Nice work, Psychology 101.' A fly is buzzing at the window; throwing itself against the clear glass.

Louisa follows my gaze. She leans across and slides open the window, but the fly stays where it is. 'Idiot,' she mutters. She turns back to me and delivers her piece de resistance: 'But really you're grieving for the father you never met.'

'You can't grieve for someone you've never met.'

Louisa puts the other half of the brownie in her mouth. 'Yes, you can,' she says with her mouth full.

There is a loud static sound in my ears. I shake my head, but it won't budge. *Leave, Grace. Walk away*. But the ringing keeps getting louder. It cuts off my brain from the rest of my body. 'Anyway, don't lecture me about mothers.'

'What is that supposed to mean?'

'You're so worried about yours finding out about your social work course, but you're fine with the fact that you're hiding your relationship with Brett. Do you know what? It's insulting for him.'

Louisa sighs dramatically. 'That's right, Grace, change the subject. But for your information, Brett's fine with it.'

'If you say so.'

'He's going overseas in less than a month. What is the point?'

'The point is the message you're giving him. Are you embarrassed about him? Is it because he's white?'

'Grace –'

'You're basically saying he's not good enough for your mother and he's not important enough to you.'

'Nobody's good enough for my mother, least of all me.'

'But it doesn't bother you.'

A noise coming from the sitting room makes Louisa look up. The fear in her eyes makes me spin around. Brett walks past me and dumps two bags of beers on the counter. He leaves the kitchen without a word or a glance.

Louisa glares at me and follows him. A few seconds later I hear Brett say, 'She's right, Louisa.'

'She's not, Brett, she's full of shit.'

A door bangs.

'Brett!' Louisa runs after him but with a squeal and squelch of wheels Brett reverses out of the drive. Louisa reappears, her eyes terrified. 'You've fucked up your life and now you're trying your hardest to fuck up mine. I love Brett, Grace. I want to be with him forever. And now he's left.' She starts crying.

'Louisa –'

'Fuck off!' she shouts and disappears into her room. Her door bangs shut.

I'm trying to decide what to do when her door opens again and she passes me with a bag slung over her shoulder. It seems stuffed with clothes. The kitchen door slams shut behind her.

Louisa's words echo through the suddenly empty house. I pick up a chocolate brownie from the tin and hold it between my fingers. It is still fresh enough for my fingers to sink into the spongy base. I bring it millimetres away from my nose and inhale. Mrs Cele uses white, milk and dark chocolate in her recipe. The butter-sugar-cocoa smell travels around my body, all the way back into sun-saturated, full-tummied little-girl memories. I step down on the pedal bin, break off the corner of the brownie, bring it up to my open mouth and drop it into the bin. I continue until it's all gone. My palms are covered in chocolatey crumbs. I hold them in front of my face, breathe in deeply then scrub them clean in the sink.

'Enough,' I tell myself. I have to get out of the kitchen – it is full of our fight. As I pass between the counter and the fridge, my arm knocks against something. I turn around at the crash. A mess of glass and water on the floor. I bend down to pick up the smooth curve of the handle. Splinters and larger chunks lie around me, rippling out from my feet. How can something that solid smash into such tiny pieces? Why go to the trouble of making something that breaks so easily?

I pick up the bag at my feet and leave the glass in the kitchen. Outside the warmth feels as thick as the mist was this morning. For a while it is enough to lean against the sliding door and feel the glare of the sun on my closed lids. But the shock of the car and our fight leaves my legs threatening to buckle and I slide down the glass until I'm sitting on the mattress.

Louisa will come back. She'll find Brett and calm him down. When they return we'll throw the bag into a bush somewhere and forget about it. We only have three days left here; Spook and his bag have done enough damage. We're teenagers for God's sake, we're here to have fun.

A car passes, music blaring from its open windows. The silence it leaves behind feels deeper and threatening. I search for the sound of the waves but even they are distant and muted. I feel for my phone in my pocket. For the first time since leaving Cape Town I wish Mum would call.

How can Spook leave fifty thousand rand and a gun behind and not return for it? Unless he stole it and was trying to get rid of it. But that doesn't make any sense because by leaving it here, he's implicating himself. It would be far easier to simply chuck the bag in the sea.

I yawn and curl onto my side.

Louisa's words won't leave me alone. The only thing more unbelievable than her conspiracy theories is the truth. It wasn't Rory so much as that horrible broom-cupboard office of his that kept me going back. It was the only place that I felt able to breathe. Until the day Rory basically dumped me, asked me not to come back. '*I'm not making you any better, Grace. I can't sit back and watch you die. I don't know what to do. You need to see somebody else.*' He didn't even have the balls to look me in the eye.

Now Spook's gone and so has Louisa. If I could leave too I would. I reach for the bag and shake it until the money inside makes a flat cushion. I smile at the absurdity of resting my head on fifty thousand rand and shut myself off from the awful afternoon.

I wake up shivering, coiled into a tight ball. For a moment I hover, beyond the reach of the past few hours. It's the dogged silence that reminds me. It must be approaching evening. The breeze is dry and fractious. My joints ache as though I've been sleeping with everything tensed. I pick up my phone to call Louisa but then stop. She'll be back later, once she's calmed down.

Despite the wind the beach is busy with walkers and dogs. I have a sudden urge to call out to them for the simple act of them stopping to acknowledge me but even if they heard my voice I'd be invisible from so far away. My stomach reminds me that I haven't eaten all day. I mentally scan the contents of the fridge and then the kitchen cupboards but the decision of what to have feels exhausting. Besides, the glass is still scattered over the kitchen floor, like a field full of landmines.

Nonetheless, this silence is beginning to gnaw. It needs pushing back with some positive action. A bath will make some noise and fill up the empty evening before Louisa returns.

As I'm walking down the passage with my towel and toiletry bag, a sound makes me jump. 'Don't be a moron, Grace,' I say out loud, then regret it. My voice sounds weird. The noise returns, like a key scratching against glass. I walk around the house methodically closing the windows and doors. The sound could have been anything, perhaps it didn't even happen. I could lock the doors to be sure – but what about when Louisa comes back? And what about the bag – do I leave it outside again? If those guys come back they'll take it and leave. But what if they don't? If I lock myself in the house and they do break in I'll have no way of escaping.

'Chill, Grace,' I say, trying to sound as confident as Mum. 'That shit doesn't happen in real life.' But it does – there is a real-life gun in a bag on my bed; real-life gangsters came snooping around the house. And what would they do if they found me alone?

I leave the sliding door unlocked but let the blinds down. If anyone tried coming into the kitchen they'd find the floor covered in glass. I feel like a stowaway stuck in this little house on stilts. What about some music? But I'd prefer to hear somebody arriving. Is it better or worse to be surprised by your attackers?

I walk into Louisa's room and sit down on the spot where I was lying this morning. The room still smells vaguely of her shampoo. Her large stripy toiletry bag is lying open on the bed. There is a full month's supply of her pill, arranged day by day – Monday, Tuesday, Wednesday – I run my finger over them. So many days! So many ordered days, so nondescript that they have to be named to make any differentiation. *Please come back now, Lou.* But her face cream and toothbrush are missing. What if she doesn't? How will I survive all night alone?

Next to the bag is the box of Myprodol. For the relief of headaches, muscular pain and period pain. The box feels reassuringly heavy but when I take out the two trays, one is empty. Mum left an article on my bed about the dangers of becoming addicted to Myprodol. It was to back up one of her 'your body is its best healer' rants. Somebody died after taking too many. What I find ironic is that it wasn't the addictive codeine that killed them, it was everyday, ordinary paracetamol.

Back in the bathroom I stand in front of the mirror. My chopped blonde hair looks rumpled, like a dirty mop. The side of my cheek carries the pattern of the bag on it. I exhale on the glass to fog it up, until there's nothing left of me, then wipe it clean. I come back slightly separated. Two Graces, or one divided? I can't tell.

I shake my head and try to blink away the double vision. It's as if I have peeled off my top layer and am watching myself from the other side of the mirror. The me I've left behind looks exposed. Her eyes are big and sad. She seems to want something from me. *What is it? Don't look at me like that*. Still she stares.

'You'll never have cheekbones,' the separated self says to me. It's cruel to come out with that now, but it's true. 'No matter how thin you get.' It would make a good farewell note: *Sorry, but I couldn't go on without any cheekbones.*

Of course, being dead, cheekbones are one thing that I would have. That's funny. Don't laugh, Grace. Death is no laughing matter. Isn't it? I'd like to die laughing. Who wouldn't?

Tears. I watch them collecting in the corner of my eyes, making rivulets down my cheeks. Some people look pretty when they cry. I look ugly. Needy. I'm exhausted from pretending to be OK. From being a 'worry'. I watch myself pick up the tray of pills and start on the top left hand corner. I've never been able to start a pack in the middle. It's too messy.

'What are you doing?' says the me on the other side of the mirror.

'I want to sleep,' I reply. I have to sleep. I cannot be awake all night, jumping at every tiny noise. I look at myself after taking two. Then I start methodically working my way through the pack.

'Two might make you sleepy but you've had eight . . . ten . . . twelve.'

'Leave me alone, for fuck's sake,' I say to myself in the mirror. My voice sounds old. I pick up the toothpaste holder and throw a cup of water at myself, but the watery, scowling me is still there.

'Go away!' I shout and swing open the door of the cabinet so that it bangs against the wall. 'Stay there!'

By the time I've reached the end of the tray, my throat feels small and tight. I sip at some water but don't want to drink too much in case I start feeling full.

The phone rings, so loudly and unexpectedly that I drop the plastic glass into the sink. Is it Spook? The question comes from the very core of me, deep inside the mess of veins and muscle tissue so that it is impossible not to think it and yet I wish I hadn't. The wish is so strong that my throat constricts. It's not Spook of course, it's bloody Mum. I flip it to silent. *Spook is gone, idiot. Lou is gone. Everyone's gone.* This empty, hollow house feels graveyard cold.

I bend down to switch on the bath taps and sit down on the loo to watch the water. It's an old enamel bath, with two large rust patches on the bottom. The water splutters and spits as it leaves the two wide-mouthed taps. Once the bath is wrist-deep I lean forward and swirl my hand around to mix up the hot and cold. I blink as I try to follow the course of my hand. It is as though my hand is actually inside my head, mixing up my thoughts each time I try and make sense of any of them.

The plug is connected to the thin metal chain but the chain

is not attached to the bath. It has come adrift. An anchor without a boat. *You and me both, Mr Plug.* No cheekbones and entirely adrift, Rory. The thing is, *Rory*, your shitty little office was my mooring. You cast me adrift.

Our final Life Skills session: Rory stands in front of our year, with a new hairstyle, dispensing nuggets of wisdom. He allows himself a meaningful pause and looks around the room. 'If you take anything from today into the rest of your lives, it's this: be curious.' I'm curious to know what he's doing tonight, whether if he knew that I was here, he'd rush in. *I can't sit back and watch you die, Grace.* Where are you tonight then? Where is anybody?

I step into the bath. It is deep and warm.

'For now,' the water replies. 'I'm warm for now.'

I lie back and feel the calm I've been hoping for. Now is all I need.

I'm on the beach next to Mum. She's lying on her tummy, her floppy green hat hiding her head and neck. I've a handful of sand above her legs and watch it trickle down. It scatters in all directions as it hits her skin. Mum's legs are always smooth. She uses a man's Gillette razor. The sand elicits no reaction from the green hat so I start up and down her legs in a method I'd seen on TV.

After a minute the hat laughs. 'What are you doing?'

'Swedish massage,' I reply, increasing the speed and intensity of my chopping hands.

'Ow! It hurts!'

'It needs to hurt,' I reply.

Louisa would get milk up her nose. God, it was funny. It

didn't matter that she did it every day.

I used to make a Father's Day card each year, put it in an envelope and address it to 'Dad'. I'd post it, even though it had nowhere to go. Mum caught me doing it one year. Her face was like a wild animal, fiery and fearful. But she caught that look and said, 'Let's get a milkshake.' I didn't make any more after that.

Why am I thinking of these things? I feel as though my brain has short-circuited and it's throwing out random thoughts. I made Rory blush once. It was at the end of a session. I had opened the door to leave. 'You're the best part of my day,' I said. I was being sarcastic, obviously, but he blushed. And because he blushed, I found myself blushing too. God, it was awful. 'I'm joking!' I said in a high voice and shut the door. I still feel embarrassed about that, but lying here in the bath, it's sort of funny.

Am I talking aloud or in my head? It sounds like stereo – one voice, two outlets.

I push myself forward towards the taps and it feels like moving through a deep, dark pool. As I switch on the hot tap, the water laughs. 'Told you,' it says.

'Not long now,' I reply, 'it's almost bedtime.'

Just when I think I am already asleep, Rory comes into the bathroom and sits on the loo.

'Well, this is a surprise,' I say. 'I thought you wanted nothing to do with me.' I should sit up – after all I'm naked.

He's looking grim. 'This is exactly what I was afraid of,' he says.

'Does it feel good to be proven right?'

He shakes his head.

'Thank you for coming,' I say, and I mean it, but he's gone.

It is tiring, being here, but not. When I get out I'll be very wrinkled. I used to dare myself to stay in until I wrinkled up to the point that I started shrivelling but the cold always got the better of me.

Slowly the room starts to fill with people, some of them teachers and pupils from school. Where is Louisa? They stand around me looking worried, talking, but too softly for me to hear. Suddenly I spot Louisa but she is facing away from me, talking to Simon Cowell. 'What is the secret to Lace's phenomenal success?' Simon asks her in a loud voice. Louisa bats away the compliment. She's wearing my glove as well as hers. 'It's all about the music.'

I try to lift my head, but a thick crushing force keeps me down. It's as though they don't even see my lying here. 'I'm awake!' I shout, pushing against the heavy pressure, but I can't move. Dido's Lament seems to be pouring out of the taps: 'Death invades me, Death is now a welcome guest.'

Suddenly I have a thought, as intense as electric shock. It is a buzzing, a push, a heave of will. I want to be in my bed. The cold water has won again. I see myself getting up. It is more like a lunge because I feel dizzy and I grab onto the towel rail to steady myself. I climb out the bath, look around for my towel and find instead a thick nightgown. I disappear into it as I wrap it around me. My room. My bed. Under my duvet it is gloriously warm. Gracie Fields stands over me and sings the Christopher Robin song slowly and softly. Now I can close my eyes. At last I can let go.

I'm still in the bath! I can't sleep yet; I'm still in the bath.

Running. Feet, breath, blood all keeping to the same rhythm.

I am the rhythm.

For a while I am nothing more than the blood in my ears, I am inside my body. Each impact of my trainers on the ground sends reverberations around my body, sharp ripples that spill into each other. But there is no pain. I sense it but I feel nothing. The ground I am running on is hard but I'm running next to the sea. I'm running in and through smudges of blue. It feels endless which is good because I could run forever. There is something on my back. Ah – Rory. Wow, he's heavy. His legs are wrapped around my waist and his arms clinging around my neck so tightly he's going to throttle me soon. His Prego-roll breath is sharp and fresh. 'This is futile, Grace. You think you're saving yourself but you're making it worse. The longer you carry this stuff around with you, and the older you get, the more burdensome it becomes.'

Really, Rory? Watch this: with a flick of my head, Rory and his blabbering mouth peel off my back with the ease of a sticky note and a pleasing *shlick* sound. Rory floats away over the sea. That's better. I am lighter and stronger without him yabbering in my ear.

Sometimes I feel so light that I leave the ground, but that makes me dizzy. I prefer the reassuring thud of trainer on the hard sand.

Mum has joined me. Dammit – how does she keep up? And she's smiling that saccharine smile of hers that could lead to homicide. Never once has she complained that I ruined her life, never once. Because everything's fine, we're always fine. *No, we're not, Mum! We're not OK, just admit it! I was a mistake; in terms of your hopes and dreams, I was a disaster.*

What? Mum's smile fades. Her pace slows.

Admit it! I shout. *I don't mind!* I start laughing, it seems funny.

Mum starts falling behind. 'Grace!' she shouts but I don't look back. Another layer gone, *shlick*. Lighter and stronger. Mum flies backwards and away from me. Perhaps she will bump into Rory.

I am pure and strong. Nothing will stop me.

A noise behind me makes me glance backwards. The scenery has changed. I am somewhere industrial. The blue smudges have become grey. I look behind. A car. The black car. I pick up my pace but it's gaining on me. As it comes alongside, the driver opens his window and grins at me. He is wearing reflective sunglasses. I see my face in them. It makes me scared. There is a turning ahead. *Turn, Grace.* The light has changed. It's darker and damper but I can keep going. There is no pain. The road narrows, the grey smudges on either side become buildings, the tops of them touching the sky, blocking out the air around me. Another corner. *Turn.* It is a narrow lane now. I can hear the car behind me. *Turn again.* The noise of the car is louder now, or perhaps it is echoing through the streets. How does it fit down these narrow paths? They are no wider than a pavement. The buildings are too tall; the light can't get in. The car is getting louder. *Run, Gracie, run.* Another corner. *Hurry.* Ahead is a tall brick wall. There's a door. Stairs leading down. You always wake before you reach the bottom. If you reach the bottom, it means you're dead.

This is it, then. This is the end.

TUESDAY

I feel hideous. 'I'm going to be sick!' I want to say, but there isn't enough time. A warm pressure, perhaps a hand, presses into the base of my spine. The warmth spreads up my back. I can feel it ripple into my veins and jump-start my synapses.

I cannot shake the sensation of flying and try to keep absolutely still. Perhaps I have left my body and am now an enlightened being. That would piss Mum off. My second name is Ariadne. Something about a string.

My eyelids feel plastered shut. I have no inclination to try and open them – there is quite enough going on in my head already. What is that smell? People underestimate smell.

If only I could stop the flying, I could finish a thought. Is it possible to fly without moving? I feel both very still and out of control.

Although if I finished a thought I'd have to move on to the next one. That feels potentially dangerous. I sense shadows of bad thoughts circling just beyond. Thoughtlessness is supposed to be negative; I think it's pretty wonderful.

That's right, there was a maze. String and a maze. Or is that Hansel and Gretel?

'String and a maze? What?'

A male voice? I thought I was alone. This is so surprising it may be worth opening my eyes for. Carefully. But the light is so bright that instinctively I roll my head to the side. Spook is next to me. Spook? No, that doesn't seem right. 'Ariadne.' I answer his question but I'm not sure whether I've said it out loud or in my head. I close my eyes again. Better. Ariadne was the Mistress of the Labyrinth. She gave Theseus a ball of string so that he could defeat a monster and find his way through the maze. Then Theseus repaid her kindness by leaving her sleeping on the beach and sailing off. Ungrateful sod.

I am so hot I would like to peel off my skin. I imagine it would come off quite easily, like a *naartjie**. I've figured out the smell in my nose: old clothes in a black bag. Seaweed. Three best smells ever would have to be toasted cheese, fresh coffee and Mum's perfume. Three worst smells: Rory's office, hospital cleaning fluid and damp sports kit. The smell in this car comes pretty close.

There is a recurring rattle. Something has come loose. It makes me open my eyes and roll my head very carefully to the side. Spook is still here; one hand on the steering wheel, his other elbow resting against the closed window. So we

* tangerine

are driving. He coughs and sniffs, rubs his nose. From what I can see without having to move, we are surrounded by mountains. Where is the sea? It's as if I'm not here. I close my eyes. Maybe I'm not; maybe when I open them again I will be somewhere else.

No, I am still here. Pity. I look down. I'm strapped into my seat. No wonder I'm hot – I'm wearing my grey tracksuit pants and Spook's jumper. That's odd, because yesterday I was wearing –

There is a song playing. I'm sure I know it. 'Is that Jake Bugg?' I ask. My mouth is dry; the words come out with the grating sound of a saw.

Spook snorts. 'Rodriguez.' He does not look at me.

'Sugar daddy,' I say.

Spook laughs. 'Sugar Man, not sugar daddy.'

When I open my eyes again there is a large green signboard ahead but the words are too smudged to read. I blink to sort them out but by then it is too late. The effort of focusing on the board makes me feel ill. 'Stop!' I say, and clamp my hand over my mouth. Spook swerves and jerks to a stop at the side of the road.

Outside it's hot and dry and I feel better immediately. With the act of moving I seem to return fully to my body. I lean over and try to puke but there is nothing there. I stand back up. Slowly the rest of the world comes back into focus. I can taste the earth in my parched mouth. We are in a flat, green valley. Vineyards. Mountains surround us on all sides, folding in on each other. I want to stay out here in the sunshine, in

157

the fresh air. I want to sit down and pick up a handful of sand and rub it together between my palms, to lie down and cover myself in the dusty earth.

'Come on,' calls Spook.

As I turn back, I notice we are not travelling in Spook's car. This one is a white station wagon. Unbelievably, it seems in worse condition than his.

Spook is pulling off even before my door is properly closed.

'Whose car is this?' I ask.

'Borrowed it.'

This car is so old that it has those wind-down windows. I open mine as far as it will go and stick my hand out, to keep a hold on the outside world. 'You came back,' I say, turning to him.

From Spook's expression I could be speaking Russian. 'Do you want to explain the empty packet of Myprodol, Grace, and the broken glass all over the kitchen?'

I shake my head and look away. No thanks. After Theseus's heartless desertion Ariadne went on to marry Dionysus, the god of wine. Ha! Karma.

Spook looks at me. 'For God's sake, close your window,' he mutters. He drums his fingers on the steering wheel and shifts about in his seat.

Mountains and vineyards. The only vineyards I know are around Franschoek and Paarl, north of Cape Town. I can't imagine any vineyards around Baboon Point. Is he taking me home? Hospital? No, no, no, not there, Spook, please. I turn to him, to talk him out of it, but his phone rings. He picks up the call and listens for a moment. He sighs. 'Fine,' he says and hangs up without saying goodbye.

He rubs the side of his face. 'I found you passed out in the bath.'

Enough, Spook.

'That was after I cut my feet open on the kitchen floor.'

'You should wear shoes more often,' I manage but my heart has contracted at his words to the point that I feel my blood stop in my veins. I turn away from him and look on the blur of passing fields. This is not the Spook I know. This is a guy yelling at me in a horrible-smelling car. Maybe going home wouldn't be such a bad thing.

'I couldn't wake you up, Grace. When I got you out of the bath, you were shivering. Then you puked all over me.'

I look down at my hands. Now I see the dirt wedged into my fingernails. But his words trigger nothing inside. I try to retreat back into those drifting, unfinished thoughts before Spook opened his mouth but they won't have me back.

'Do you know how easily you could have drowned?'

'Stop it.' I watch the digital clock on the dashboard, waiting for fifty-nine to flick to zero, which in turn will free the eleven to change to twelve o'clock. But it won't move. I feel Spook's eyes flicking between me and the road, waiting for me to say something, but I stare fixedly ahead. A lorry transporting new cars approaches us and behind it a Greyhound bus. That would make a horrible crash.

Spook bangs the steering wheel. 'Do you have any idea how stupid that was? Where was Louisa?'

'Stop shouting.'

'I thought you were dead!' He shouts even louder. He takes a deep breath, then says in a very controlled voice: 'Where is Louisa?'

I shake my head. 'She went after Brett. They had a fight.'
Caused by me.

'But she was gone all night and she didn't answer her phone.'

I shrug, as if I'm as confused as he is.

The next time we pass a green board, I catch the words 'Riversdale 10'. 'Riversdale? I thought you were taking me home.' We are a long way from Cape Town, travelling in the opposite direction. We're on our way to the East Coast.

For some reason Spook finds this funny.

'Not hospital, please. Just drop me back at my house.'

'Not going to happen.'

'Why not?'

'I have an errand to run.'

'Where?'

'Mossel Bay.' He seems irritated with me for being here, but he brought me along.

A few valleys later Spook looks at me again. 'How do you feel?'

'Fine,' I lie. My stomach is cramping. I have no control over where I am or where I'm going. I wish I could make myself pass out again.

'Drink this,' he says and reaches down into the side pocket of his door and pulls out a bottle of Energade. It's warm.

I shake my head.

'Grace,' he growls.

'I'll be sick,' I say. I'm five years old again, swaying with fever, pleading with my mum who is trying to force more medicine down.

'Take small sips.'

I do as he says, although it makes me want to cry. The explosion of sugar in my mouth is so intense that for a moment I am going to be sick. But my body lets me down. It grabs at the taste, desperate for more.

The music has stopped. We are driving through a wide, flat valley. Long, grassy bushes line the road. Every now and then we pass a cluster of farm buildings in the distance. The mountains that we were driving alongside have shrunk to a gentle wave-like shape, a darker shade of blue than the sky. I shift in my seat to relieve my aching bum, and undo the seatbelt. I have to get rid of the jumper. Underneath it I'm wearing a white vest top. I blush as I realise he must have had to dress me. A fresh tide of nausea washes up through me. Somehow I need to manage to go for a run today. Yes, a run. Even the thought of it makes me feel calmer.

As I turn to chuck the jersey onto the back seat I catch sight of the navy rucksack. It reminds me of something, something urgent, but I blink at it a few moments. I glance at Spook and then back at the bag. The money. The gun. What is the matter with me? How could I have forgotten? Now that I think about it, that bag is responsible for everything that has gone wrong. And everything is wrong. I am stuck in a strange car with a gun, a bag of cash and a man of no fixed address, driving in the wrong direction. Tears spill over my cheeks. I don't wipe them away, hoping that in the silence Spook won't notice. But there are so many of them that it becomes too hard to keep them quiet. I cover my face in my hands and sob, as if I'm getting rid of all the cold bathwater.

Crying doesn't make me feel any better but at least Spook doesn't say anything. I sniff loudly. I fix my gaze on a smudge of bird poo on the windscreen and swallow back the second round of tears. 'Why do you have a gun?'

Spook rubs the back of his head. He stretches his neck from side to side.

'Louisa says everyone is South Africa has a gun but that's not true. No one in my family does.' My words are met with silence, broken only by the unidentified rattle. 'And don't tell me it's only for self-defence; look at freaking Oscar. If you're not going to use it then why have it?'

'I didn't say I wasn't going to use it.'

'What?'

Spook sighs and shakes his head. 'There are things about this world that you don't get if you're eighteen and have been living all your life in a nice house with Mummy.'

His patronising tone makes me want to hit him. 'What happened to "I'm just a Rousseau-quoting, ocean-loving hippy?"'

'I never claimed to be a hippy. Sounds like you have stuffed me into a very small box because I like to surf.'

I turn and stare out of the window. We are travelling through an endless succession of rolling hills, surrounded by yellow fields. Each of the dips in this suspension-less car makes my stomach turn over. Every time we near the top of a rise, I cling to the brief hope that surely on the other side the scenery will change, but it never does. Despite what he says, on Sunday Spook *was* the ocean-loving hippy. This Spook is somebody else. Should I be worried about being in this car with him?

* * *

At last we are approaching the coast and Mossel Bay. Giant oil refineries spread out on either side of the national road. It is funny how people associate Mossel Bay with the start of the world-famous Garden Route when its approach is so ugly. We leave the highway but before we descend into the town Spook turns at a sign that says 'D'Almeida'. I look at him, thinking he's made a mistake, but the fixed look on his face keeps me quiet. What is he doing driving into a township?

The road winds slowly up a hill. Streets peel off to the side. They are lined with identical blocks of flats. Each block has an external staircase at the front of the building. The newer buildings are painted mustard yellow, the older ones were once white. Graffiti covers the ground floor of the buildings. Washing hangs from the top floor between the buildings and across the road. The roads are so uniform that I imagine a town planner, sitting at his desk with a pencil and ruler. But in a manner that would annoy the planner enormously, boxy lean-to houses have mushroomed up in almost every free space. Some have marked out a backyard with corrugated iron walls; others are no more than shacks. Kids and dogs spill out into the street. Minivan taxis crawl up and down the road, hovering to pick up and drop off passengers. I close my eyes. After the silence and emptiness of the past few hours it is too much to take in.

When I look again, the houses are bigger and further apart. Some of them have gardens, with straggly creepers spilling over the side of the Vibracrete walls. Spook turns into a smaller road. A few of the houses are double-storey, with high walls and barbed wire running along the top. Spook pulls up outside a high brick wall, and sighs. 'Don't go anywhere, I won't be long.' He leans back for the bag, unzips it and takes out the gun. He wraps it in a T-shirt that had been lying on the seat then leans over me, opens the glove compartment and chucks it in.

'What if someone –' I start but he's already out of the car. He walks up a short drive, opens a solid steel gate and closes it behind him.

I rest my feet against the glove box. Three days ago I was sitting in exactly the same position, only next to Louisa, driving through Lambert's Bay. The street is deserted. My stomach is cramping. I sniff and feel tears close by. I lift my hand to wipe my nose and see that it's shaking. That makes me feel worse. I take hold of my hand with the other but suddenly I'm shaking all over. No matter how far I burrow into the seat I can't stop it. My senses are all messed up – I'm cold and hot at the same time. I sniff again and force myself to concentrate on something outside. The only experiences I have of townships are the ones outside Cape Town where we planted trees and painted murals as part of our outreach projects at school. This is different. It feels like a suburb with a township plonked on top of it. I pick up Spook's phone and scroll through his songs for something to do. Nirvana. Radiohead. Some weird trance stuff. Jesus Christ. *Come on, Spook!*

There is a playground further down the road. The merry-go-round is full of teenagers. Why aren't they at school? A couple of smaller kids in school uniform play on the slide. A dishevelled middle-aged man is sitting on the only unbroken swing. I rest my head back on the seat and close my eyes. That brings back the dizzy feeling. When Louisa arrives back to find both me and the bag missing, she's going to go ape-shit. I hope Spook left her a message because I can't face explaining this to her. I wouldn't know what to say.

There is a girl walking towards me. She is wearing tight purple hot pants, and a white T-shirt vest that struggles over her boobs. Her thighs cushion out from the shorts. If she were white, her thighs would look terrible with all that pale, veiny flesh, but somehow she looks ripe. Is she a prostitute? Do prostitutes work in the day? As she nears me she catches my glance in the mirror. Her expression isn't hostile, but it's definitely a 'what are you doing here?' look. I blush and sink lower into my seat. Once she's past I squeeze down the lock on the door.

Where is Spook? What is taking him so long? Why has he left me in the car, like a dog, guarding a gun?

The hot pants girl has settled on a white plastic chair on the pavement in front of the next-door house. Another girl in a shiny blue tracksuit walks up to her. They talk for a while, they laugh. Tracksuit sits down on Hot Pants' lap. Tracksuit says something, which makes Hot Pants shriek and push her off. A boy rides by on a bicycle. He slows down as he passes them and yells something I don't catch. Hot Pants shouts in indignation. 'Your mother!' she yells after him, which makes me smile.

The minutes seem to pass in slow motion, as if everything is happening under water. Women pass with Shoprite bags, kids on their way home from school cluster around each other. A car drives by. The world seems heavy with the weight of everybody going about their business. A door bangs on the other side of the wall. I swivel around in my seat, hoping to see Spook, but no one appears. As I turn back, a black car is pulling up, directly in front of me. It's the car that followed Louisa and me on the Main Road, the car that I saw on my walk with Spook, the car that came to the house.

The sluggishness gives way to a high-pitched alarm in my head. Where the fuck is Spook? A man gets out from the driver's seat; he looks over at the girls. They return his gaze but with none of their earlier banter. He glances at our car. Then he looks at me and stops in recognition. He is small and scrawny, like an old piece of rope. He saunters over to the driver's side. With his arm resting on the roof, he bends down and knocks on the closed window. In his mirrored aviator sunglasses I see a glimpse of myself. Wide-eyed. When he lifts them onto his head, his eyes are small, hiding behind creases of skin. There is a tattoo down the side of his neck, letters I can't make out. He lifts his chin and knocks again. I can't ignore him; he'd probably break the window. I unwind it, my hands slipping over the plastic handle.

'*Lekker* flas' new wheels,' he comments.

Although I keep my eyes fixed ahead, I can feel him studying me. 'Where's Gavin?' His breath smells of tobacco and gum.

I swallow. 'Who?' The girls are watching us. Would they help me if this guy did something?

'Don't be cute.'

'You mean Spook?'

This amuses him. 'If you say so.'

I point in the direction of the steel gate.

He takes his time to consider this, then straightens up and stretches his arms above his head. His torso is skinny; his baggy jeans show red underpants and a slash-shaped scar above his belly button.

He glances towards the house, then leans inside to unlock the door. He sits down next to me. My stomach heaves impotently. He reaches towards me and fingers the silver 'G' pendant on my necklace. 'Pretty,' he says. 'Is Gavin your boyfriend?'

'What?' It takes me a moment to follow his train of thought. 'He's twice my age.'

He leans towards me. 'Some like it old.'

I picture the gun inside the glove box, less than a metre away from me. *Don't be ridiculous, Grace.* I tuck my hands under my bum.

'Don't be scared of me.' He leans closer. 'I'm not the bad guy, I'm jus' the messenger. The *bad* guys are behind that there wall.' His laugh is high-pitched, like the jackals in *The Lion King*.

'Why are they bad?' I ask. I'm as surprised by my question as he is. Am I crazy? I stare straight ahead.

He tuts at my question. 'They're only bad if you fuck with them. But you look like a good little girl.'

I try to swallow, but my throat is too constricted.

'See, your boyfriend took what didn't belong to him. So in actual fact, he's the bad guy.' He laughs again and moistens his lips with his tongue. '*Vooitog*,' he says. I look down.

---

* Shame

167

A phone rings, a tinny version of 'Where have you been all my life?' He fishes it out of a back pocket, and listens for a moment while watching me. But when he replies, his tone is different. 'What? Where must I now go? *Jirre**. Why me?' His voice is whiny. 'Ja, OK, gotcha.' He hangs up and leans towards me. 'Tell Gavin to stop fucking with the big boys,' he says, then disappears.

The driver's door is still open when Spook reappears. I've been meaning to close it, but my hands are still tucked under my thighs and my arms seem incapable of moving. Spook gets back in the car and bangs the door shut. He looks back over his shoulder as he reverses. The car hiccups and jolts as he misses the gear change.

After three blocks I look at him. 'Gavin.'

Spook wipes the sweat off his face with his T-shirt. He doesn't register that I've spoken. He swallows a few times then wipes his face again.

As we turn out of D'Almeida, I clear my throat. 'Your name is *Gavin*,' I say loudly.

Spook does not reply.

'So while you were catching up with your buddies inside, this guy, this gangster guy comes up and gets into the car, sits down next to me and, and touches my necklace, and is saying he's not the bad guy, you're the bad guy and by the way your name is *Gavin*. He could have done *anything* to me!' My voice hurts from shouting.

Finally Spook looks at me. He seems surprised that I'm there.

* Jesus

168

Something snaps inside. I have spent too long in this car that smells of old men. I need space. I open my door. Air and dust and car fumes rush up at me.

'What the fuck!' Spook swerves around an oncoming car, at the same time trying to lean across me.

'Let me out!'

'Shut the door!'

'Not until you tell me what's going on.' I have to shout over the noise of the car.

'Dammit Grace! Close the door.' Spook pulls to a halt on the side of the road.

My hands are shaking. I feel out of control.

Spook sits back and rubs his eyes. 'They're not gangsters, Grace. They're poachers.'

'Same difference. Anyway, what does that have to do with you?' Nothing makes sense today.

'I needed the money.'

'For what?'

Spook looks at me like I'm stupid. 'To live.'

'You're an abalone poacher?'

He doesn't reply, not because he feels bad or angry, he simply doesn't care either way. We sit in silence on the side of the road, while an endless procession of cars stop-start past us. I wait for my heart to slow, wait for his words to make sense.

After a few minutes he adds: 'I poached in the wrong patch.'

'What?'

'They "own" that area of coastline. I took a chance. Thought I'd got away with it.'

169

If only he'd left me in the bath, I would have woken up and gone to bed.

'The money was for them,' I say needlessly, trying to make sense of everything. But as hard as I try, I can't picture Spook as a poacher. 'So that's it, you've paid them back, they'll leave you alone now?'

'Why wouldn't they?' snaps Spook. With this comment he jumps back into action. He picks up his phone, types a message, then starts the car. He forces his way back into the traffic and turns up the radio. This day has turned out far worse than I could ever have imagined. But at least we're going home.

I think back to Mum and Julia's argument about poaching. How ironic – here I am next to an actual poacher and he doesn't give a shit about either 'social upliftment' or 'entrapment'. He simply wanted to make some money.

It's as though I'm sitting at the optometrist wearing those funny glasses. As soon as something comes into focus, the lens is changed and everything returns to being blurry. Nothing about Spook or Gavin or whoever he is, is true. I bite down hard on my bottom lip as the realisation settles. How could I have believed him? But it's worse than that – I believed *in* him. I believed in a guy who had chosen to live outside the 'chains' of society; who had found a better way. My fingernails dig into my palms. And the surfing! Sitting on the board, half-frozen from the cold, spellbound by his connection, his *devotion* to the sea. How can he plunder the thing he loves the most? 'People come into your life for a reason' – one of Mum's favourite mantras. The reason Spook appeared in

170

my life was to highlight what a big fat idiot I am. The very worst of it is that if I hadn't met Spook I'd never have had that argument with Louisa; the argument that has probably ended our friendship forever. We'd be in Baboon Point, lying in the sun, being eighteen.

Spook's phone rings. He picks it up. 'Marvin.' He listens for a moment. I feel him looking at me. 'Because that's what you said. No. Jesus Christ! No, Marvin, you sort it out.'

He chucks his phone into the back seat. A moment later he bangs the steering wheel.

Closing my eyes is a mistake. It is like opening the moving car door again, this time on the events of the last day. The brownies and the pills and the bath and the stale breath of the gangster guy rush at me. I'm stuck. I'm stuck inside my head and I'm stuck inside this horrible car and inside this endless day. My palms are wet, my breath feels too thin. *Think of the beach, Gracie. Think of that lovely, long beach and the nippy air chasing you on. We're going home.*

We pass a signboard. 'Did that say Oudtshoorn?'

'Short cut,' answers Spook.

'Shorter than the N2?'

Spook grunts in reply.

That's not right. My sense of direction is rubbish but I can't see how heading north to Oudtshoorn instead of south or west counts as a short cut. Since leaving Mossel Bay we've been driving across flat green farmland. But now the road has begun to snake around *koppies* * as we start to climb out of the valley.

* small hills

171

How can a twisty, narrow road be quicker than a motorway? I glance sideways at Spook. His face is set. Every few minutes he shifts forward in his seat, as if willing the car to go faster. The car fan is on full, pumping out hot, dusty air onto which heavy male sweat clings. The claustrophobic atmosphere is giving me pins and needles in my brain.

'Can we stop?' I ask.

'Not now,' he replies. His eyes flicker towards the rearview mirror. We haven't seen another car in over ten minutes. I don't see why we can't stop. If he were in that much of a hurry he'd not have chosen this back road.

'Just for a bit? I want to –'

'No, Grace!' Spook shouts.

I jump involuntarily at the impact of his voice.

I turn away to hide the tears that have sprung up again, but somehow Spook catches them.

'Enough with the crying.' The ferociousness in his voice is neither Spook, nor Gavin. It's simply mean.

The ordered fields have taken on irregular shapes as we dip in and out of a series of valleys. Spook's gear changes around the corners are jerky, making me feel sick. I look down at my phone. No signal. 'Missing girl, eighteen, believed to be travelling with notorious poacher.'

Stop being hysterical, Grace, I hear Louisa saying in my head. The authority in her voice makes me feel more teary because the last time she'd told me I was hysterical was on the beach when I told her my suspicions about the black car. I was right.

Spook drums his fingers on the steering wheel. I feel him glance over at me. He sighs. 'We'll stop at the next petrol station.'

* * *

If the digital clock would only switch from eleven fifty-nine to twelve o'clock it would be a sign that things would turn out fine. But it sits there stubbornly holding back, keeping us locked in the mid-afternoon heat, driving around endless bends in the road. I force myself to think about something that exists outside this car. The beach. But I can't stay on the beach forever. Rory, in his short-sleeved checked shirt, leaning back into that poor, overburdened chair. 'You have such steely determination, Grace. Such willpower. You can achieve anything you put your mind to.' *I will.* Once I've got myself back home I will make things better. I will find a way to make it up to Louisa, I will convince Mum to let me do my course this year; I will come top of the class and no one will ever have to know about the Myprodol.

There is a figure standing on the hard shoulder of the road, waving a red flag as we approach a bend. 'What now?' mutters Spook and slows. We round the corner to find a long line of stationary cars ahead. Spook curses as he comes to a stop. I sip at the bottle of Energade.

A man and woman are leaning against the side of the car ahead. The man's sleeves are rolled up; he's smoking a cigarette. The woman is fanning herself with a magazine. They are both thickset and could be anything between forty and sixty years old, the type of person that would be impossible to identify in a police line-up. They ignore each other deeply the way married people do.

Spook gets out. 'What's going on, *boet*?' he calls.

The man looks up. 'Been here ten minutes already.'

Spook whistles. He crosses to the other side of the road, looking for signs of movement. The woman is silent. She studies Spook quizzically – his flip-flops, boardies and grubby T-shirt – an overgrown boy. Then she turns to me.

Spook walks back. 'D'you think it's an accident?'

The man shrugs. 'Haven't seen any cop cars come past.'

'Fuck,' says Spook and folds his arms around his head. The woman's face pinches in disapproval. Spook walks around to my side. 'You wanted to stop, so we stopped.'

I turn away from him. I feel the woman watching us.

'Suit yourself.' He shrugs and walks away. The woman says something to the man. He looks at me and also shrugs.

Spook digs around in the back of the car for his cell phone. He stares at it, seemingly reading a message. 'No, no, no,' he mutters, shaking his head. 'Get your shit together, Marvin.'

'Why are you so stressed?'

He looks at me. 'I should have left you in the bath.' He crosses to the other side of the road.

I find myself blinking repeatedly at the impact of his words. Even the woman, who has no idea what he means, looks surprised. She steps closer, flagrantly trying to get a better view of me.

I have my phone – I could ask the woman for a lift to the nearest town and call my mum. The idea seems drastic. I would have to come up with a plausible reason for not being in Baboon Point, accompanying a complete stranger on a bizarre road trip. But then again this could be the gut feeling I'll spend the rest of my life wishing I'd listened to. I look back at the woman, but she's lost interest in us and I feel my resolution waver.

Finally an overburdened lorry drives towards us at a funereal pace, followed by a long stream of cars and trucks. Ahead of us people are turning their engines back on. The woman and man climb back into their car. *This is your last chance, Grace.* I can see myself sitting in their back seat, calling my mum. But how do I know they are not a pair of psychos? It would be even madder than staying where I am. As the lorry passes us I see it is transporting cattle. Through the air vent along the side of the long trailer bovine noses stick out. Big, dark eyes look straight at me.

Spook is back in the car, muttering. I bite my lip. From the position of the overhead sun, it's obvious that we will be driving in the dark. Were it the old Spook, I'd ask him how long it should take, but I have had enough tongue lashings for one day.

A few minutes on we reach the cause of the hold-up – workers have been digging up a long stretch of the road. There is no sign of the big machines today, only a man wearing a yellow traffic vest leaning on a green sign that says '*Ry*/Go'. On the side of the road is a portable hut where two other men are chatting. One is sitting on a white plastic chair, holding a walkie-talkie. The other is sitting on a tree stump.

'Unbelievable,' Spook breaks the silence. 'Bunch of clowns.'

'They're fixing the road, earning an honest wage. Contributing to society,' I mutter.

My phone falls out of the car as I open the door. I chuck it back on the passenger seat.

'Be quick,' says Spook. I swing the car door shut. At last we've pulled into a petrol station. The afternoon sun has started to slip. But if anything, it feels even hotter. The smell of petrol seems to be rising from the concrete slabs of the forecourt. There is a small garage shop and next to that a cafe that looks like the Wimpy's poorer cousin. Apart from the two petrol *joggies** and the shop assistant, the place is deserted. I quickly dismiss my idea of phoning my mum and waiting for her here. In a few hours we'll be back at the house.

The loos are around the back of the building. I have to collect a key from the shop assistant to unlock the door. The key ring is a smooth piece of wood that has the word '*Dames***'* written on it in felt tip. The thought of all the hands touching it before mine makes me feel queasy. Inside the loo the only light comes from a barred window. It is heady with disinfectant, the floors damp in a way that makes you curl up your toes. I glance at myself in the mirror. I look shit. My eyelids are puffy from crying. My eyes seem to have withdrawn almost completely into my head.

'Awesome,' I say and turn away. As I do, I remember standing in front of the mirror last night and find I'm shivering again.

I glance at the service shop on the way back to the car. I don't suppose they sell fresh carrots. Spook is waiting in the car. There is a large packet of chips in his lap. 'Want some?'

I shake my head.

'Drink this.' He hands me another bottle of Energade.

After hurrying the petrol attendant along, he turns to me. 'I need to borrow some money.'

'I don't have my wallet here.'

---

*   attendants

**   Ladies

'It's in the glove box.'

I fish it out, trying not to touch the wrapped-up gun. 'How much?'

'Four hundred.'

'What?'

'Come on, Grace, I'm trying to get you home,' he says, not meeting my eye.

'Via Joburg. Why don't you ask them about the weird rattle while we're here?'

Spook snorts in derision. 'These guys are petrol *joggies*. What do they know about cars?'

'More than you.' My voice is braver than I feel.

We have been climbing up the edge of a valley. At times the road leads us right into the folds of the hillside so that we can't see anything but rock and overhanging trees. It is blessedly cooler. I feel able to think clearly for the first time today. I turn to ask Spook what time we'll get back, but his frown of concentration makes me decide to leave it a while. As we reach the top of the incline, we emerge out of the shadows into a different landscape. Scrub bush has replaced the farmland. The sky has softened ahead of the coming evening. We are on a plateau. Valleys fan out below us and in the far distance, a smudge of blue sea. The car makes a burping sound.

'That's not good,' I say, turning to him.

'It's fine,' he says.

'It can't be the petrol,' I say a few minutes later. Spook is chewing his lip and doesn't respond. We haven't seen another car since we left the petrol station. I have another hundred rand in my purse; I should have given that to him.

The tar road disintegrates into loose gravel, forcing Spook to slow down. He scratches his ear; he drums on the steering wheel. Soon potholes force him to weave about the width of the road.

'The road is shocking,' I say.

'Floods last winter,' he grunts without looking at me. Does he really wish he'd left me behind in the bath? Probably.

A loud pop makes Spook jerk the car to the right so that I'm pretty much sitting in the bushes.

'Shit,' says Spook. He leaves the engine running and gets out.

I turn around in my seat and see him standing at the back of the car. I wait for him to come back but when he doesn't I clamber over his seat and walk around to join him. He is standing with his arms crossed, feet apart, glowering at the back of the car.

'What is it?' I say.

'Puncture,' he replies.

The back wheel is completely flat. 'Bummer,' I say.

'D'you think?' He turns on me as if it's my fault.

'So change it,' I snap and walk away.

He starts laughing.

'What?' I turn around.

'No spare.'

'You chose this godforsaken road with no spare tyre?'

'That's right,' he answers, stony-faced.

I shiver in the silence. We're supposed to be on our way home! I wish I was anywhere in the world but here. The sounds of the bush take over, indifferent to the two pathetic creatures by the side of the road. Shushes and scurries and lazy air moving in far off trees. Above that is the sound of a low rumble. I listen to it for a while, to be sure. 'Spook?'

'Ja.' His voice is low and quiet and defeated.

'Can you hear that? There's a car coming.' Surely they'd be able to help us.

He jumps up. 'Get in the car,' he barks.

'What?'

'Get in the car!' he shouts so that I'm running to do as he says. I scramble back into my seat. He leans across me and fishes the gun out of the T-shirt.

'What are you doing? The car could help us with the tyre.'

'Stay here,' he says.

I stare after the madman who has just slammed the door. His reactions are as irrational and random as if I were flicking through late-night movie channels. Maybe he is actually unstable. 'Stop it, Grace!' I say aloud but my voice is wobbly. Then it dawns on me – the flat tyre is the last thing on Spook's mind. The call to Marvin; the text message. Something has gone wrong. The gangster/poachers are coming after us. The thought sucks the remaining air from the car. *Tell Gavin to stop fucking with the big boys.* That's why we took this bizarre route back. I picture the black car, climbing the side of the valley, getting closer all the time. *Tell me I'm wrong*, I beg Louisa, *Tell me I'm crazy*. The man with his tattooed neck and cheap cigarette breath. *Vooitog*. I find I'm holding my hands against my chest, reciting every prayer I've ever heard. *I don't want to die. I will never, ever take any painkiller again as long as I live. I'll spend my life doing good works. Just please not here, on the top of a hill, so far away from my mum.* I squeeze my eyes shut. Through my open window the approaching car sounds as though it's slowing down. 'I'm sorry I didn't pick up your calls,' I whisper.

But the car doesn't stop. When I open my eyes there's nothing more than a thick cloud of dust. For a moment I feel physically jangled, like when you prepare to take a big jump downwards but land on the same surface.

Spook opens the door. He sits down heavily in the driver's seat, watching the dust cloud left by the car dissipate reluctantly in the heavy air. He wraps up the gun and puts it away. Although his face is tightly controlled, his hands can't stop shaking.

He stares at them for a moment. He shakes his head. Then he starts laughing.

'What?'

He's laughing too much to answer. He pushes himself out of his seat. The laughter grows louder and more out of control, he's shouting and laughing at the same time. My mum told me once that she was with her granny when the police arrived to tell her that her husband had died in a car accident. Her granny had started laughing hysterically. The policeman had had to slap her to make her stop. 'Her laughter was the most horrible sound in the world,' said Mum. Watching Spook, I know what she means.

'Do you –'

'Fuck's sake,' he mutters. He kicks the wheel. 'Fuck's *sake*!' He kicks the number plate. He walks around the car, kicking the wheels and the doors. 'Stupid fucking USELESS piece of shit! Nothing works!' he turns and shouts at the hills. 'Nothing ever fucking works!' He is shouting so loudly that his voice is hoarse. 'For once, just once in my life, can't I get a break?' He yells at the sky. 'Jesus! Is it too much to ask?' He bangs his hands down on the bonnet of the car. He turns away and kicks at the stones on the side of the road. 'What did I do to deserve this . . . this SHIT?'

You're a poacher, I think, *that can't be good karma*. Then I think of the gun, wrapped up in the T-shirt in the glove compartment. Am I part of the shit he doesn't deserve?

Spook carries on muttering words that sound like nonsense, garbled up, throwing his arms around like a child having a fit in the supermarket. Finally he is spent and sits down on the side of the road, holding his head in his hands.

I start at a walk but soon I'm running. Though my flip-flops against the gravel road slow me down, it feels as good as though I'm on the beach, wild and free, barely touching the ground. I need air. I gulp it in, as if I've been underwater for the past few hours. Yes Rory, running is my *literal* escape mechanism. If only you could see me now.

My plan is simple. I will not stop. I've been sitting all day; I will run all night if I must. I snatch glances at the surrounding *veld**. We are so high up that the hills and valleys we climbed out of are barely visible. On top of the world. I feel no connection to this strange world. It is as though I'm running in a video game. The only sounds that reach me are my thumping heart and sharp intakes of breath.

---

* open country

This is the first sensible decision I've made in days. Each step is a confirmation that I am back in control. I feel my legs stretching out, my strides getting longer and firmer.

There is a battered brown road sign up ahead, slightly obscured by a bush. The signpost points towards a barely visible track that will take you to a place called Gamkaskloof. Underneath that is written, *'Die Hel'*. I could run there. It is a long time since a car has been down there. As I slow in indecision the first stab of pain hits, as sharp as a tear through my insides. I'm doubled over, panting, with my fingers digging into my sides to stop the pain. My body, normally so obedient, is in revolt – cramping and spasming, as useful as Spook's piece of shit car. I sink down to a rock underneath the sign and clutch my knees, rocking back and forth in an attempt to make it stop. It is true – I've landed up in hell.

I am left exposed and helpless. An eighteen-year-old girl stranded in the middle of nowhere. When the pain dulls, reluctantly, I am too exhausted to lift my head. Deep, otherworldly silence settles around me. Perhaps this is all a very clear dream: Spook didn't find me in the bath and I'm in a coma, experiencing a vivid alternative reality. I pinch myself hard. 'Ow!' I say aloud. But things hurt in dreams too – how can one be sure?

At the sound of footsteps I lift my head. Spook looks grey under his tanned skin. He stops in front of me and rubs the back of his head in the same way he did that first morning, looking down at me from the deck. I feel it on the inside of my palm.

'Come on.'

* Hell

'Can't we just drive with the flat tyre to the next town?' I ask.

But he dismisses it with a short 'Too far', and starts walking back to the car. A few minutes later he stops again. 'Grace!' His voice sounds like Mum's at the end of a very long day.

'Maybe there's a farmhouse at this Gamkaskloof?' I call.

'It's a fucking nature reserve,' he replies.

The sun is full and fat and slipping dangerously close to the horizon. This environment is as alien to me as a country halfway across the world. I know pavements and cars and beaches. Even the Sunday morning walks Mum and I take on the mountain are signposted. Those are circuits, with a beginning and an end.

I take out my phone. There is no signal and only 20 per cent of the battery left. No phone, no people, no car. What would Louisa do? The thought makes me laugh. In Louisa's world this would never happen.

Spook is back. 'I'm sorry.' His tone makes it clear that although he is apologising, it ought to be me.

'When Louisa and Brett get back and I'm missing along with the bag with the gun and fifty thousand rand, they are going to freak. They'll go to the police. The police will send out a search party for me.'

'I left messages for Louisa. Last night and this morning.'

This makes me feel very small. 'She could be freaking now.'

Spook's hands are in his pockets. He looks around, kicks at the stones on the road. 'You can't sit there all night.'

'I can,' I say, looking in the opposite direction. I keep my gaze steady until I hear him walking away. I will sit here all night. How long is twelve hours anyway? I'd rather sit here than tag along after a lying, poaching criminal who wishes he hadn't fished me out of the bath. I rub my arms bracingly, the way my mum used to do after I'd stayed in the pool too long. I glance up and catch the sun as it drops from view. I feel stung by its desertion.

People suffer unspeakable hardships every day – sitting on the side of the road for twelve hours is nothing compared to being forced into child slavery or crossing a nature reserve full of predatory animals in order to become a refugee in a country only marginally less bankrupt than your own. But I *am* in a nature reserve. Still, this is not the Kruger Park by any stretch of the imagination. The biggest animals around here must be buck or baboon. Snakes don't come out at night. But what about hyena, or those nasty pointy-eared *rooikat**?

Then comes the most wonderful sound in the world – a ping from my phone. I take it out and stare at it – three bars. Three bars! Angels appearing in the sky could not have made me happier. I have to call my mum. I have to speak to her. After I've dialled her number three times, each time listening to the ten rings before switching to voicemail, I have to acknowledge that she's not going to answer her phone. Why not? Where would she be at eight o'clock on a Tuesday? It's not one of her yoga nights; even if she's out, why isn't she answering? I try the landline at home.

It is answered after four rings, and I almost laugh out loud with relief. But the voice that answers doesn't belong to my mum.

'Ju-Ju?' I ask.

'Hello, Trouble.'

---

* caracal

'Why are you there? Where's Mum?' Oh dear, Mum is not going to be happy. Every now and then Ju-Ju moves in with us for a few weeks. Mum calls it the 'Julia Cycle'. Ju-Ju calls it a spot of bad luck she didn't see coming. It is normally the fault of some 'freakin' asshole'. Once she stayed for a month, until Mum told her she had the mentality of a freeloading teenager. They didn't speak for a long time after that.

'She went away for a few days, chicken. That friend of hers . . . the angry one . . . I always want to call her Chlamydia –'

I laugh. 'Clarissa!' I've never liked Clarissa. I've always had the feeling she resents having me around.

'Exactly. She said your mum needed a break and took her to some spa where you can't take cell phones . . . I forget.'

'A break? Why does she need a break? What about work?' I can't imagine Mum agreeing to taking an unplanned 'break'. Those are for people who are not fine.

There is a little silence from Julia that suggests there is something I'm being a bit thick about. 'Your mum tried to get hold of you before she left. Anyway, I'm housesitting.'

I hear her take a drag of her cigarette. 'Are you smoking inside?'

'No,' she answers quickly.

'But you're talking on the inside phone.'

'No one likes a smart aleck.'

If Ju-Ju is not having one of her moments, why is she housesitting? It seems very out of character for Mum to leave her sister alone in her home. 'Ju – are you on Gracewatch?' At around the age of eight I started resenting the word 'babysit', so Ju invented the term 'Gracewatch'.

My aunt is quiet. Now I get it – my mum wouldn't leave on a phone-free break unless there was someone around, in case of an emergency. Is she expecting an emergency? Am I the reason Mum needs a break?

'Should I be on Gracewatch?' asks Ju, after another drag.

'No!' I say, looking out over the glowing sky. 'Everything's fine.'

'Sure? What are you doing?'

'Just chilling outside. The sun has just set and left behind a beautiful sky. Anyway, I should go,' I say quickly, as I feel the tears building up. 'Bye.'

The sky *is* beautiful. Golden oranges and reds are slowly deepening into each other. From this position I could be Moses, or Moses' girlfriend, looking out over the Promised Land. It's the kind of scene that is used as a backdrop for motivational speeches: you are limitless, as free and perfect as Mother Nature. Yet I feel like the last thread that was holding me down has just snapped and I'm falling through a vast empty void. I cannot bear to be an emergency. But I feel completely lost. I've spent my life trying to find the missing pieces of myself and reasons for my being on this planet. But they don't exist. Everything is so random. The fact that I exist is random; the fact that I met Spook; that I am stuck here, in the middle of nowhere, staring up at the stars. No one is watching; whether I'm here or not makes no difference to the world or history or even the next minute.

If Rory were sitting next to me now, he'd turn to me and say: 'You are a child of the universe. No less than the trees and the stars.' The first time he quoted those words, I thought he was messing with my head. They are the words Mum would say as she kissed me goodbye every morning; they belong to a poem that sits in a frame above her bath. Even though it says 'M. Ehrmann' at the bottom I used to pretend it was a note from my dad, a letter he sent to me when I was born. Rory. If only he were sitting next to me, the rapidly darkening sky would be poetic, not threatening. I miss him and his cramped little office and his horrible pack-of-three shirts. I miss the fact that he was so big – bigger than me and Mum put together and bigger than everything I threw at him. Until the day my 'problems' became too big for Rory the giant to fix and he didn't want to see me any more. Up until this moment I have been so embarrassed every time I let myself think about that day, so ashamed that I was too bulky a problem for that huge man to carry. But tonight I feel something different – I feel desperately sad. More than sad. Perhaps Louisa is right after all – I feel as though someone in my life has died. I feel grief.

My phone rings. I snatch it up. 'Brett?'

'Grace? Hooray! It's Helen.'

'Helen?'

'Where are you, my love?'

The words make me laugh. I can't help it, exhaustion washes over me. 'I'm a long way from Baboon Point,' I say. I take a deep breath. 'Is Louisa there?' I screw up my eyes in anticipation of the conversation I have to have.

'Uh – no. She's gone back home.' Helen's voice sounds careful.

I am so disappointed I can't find any words.

'Oh my god, it's been drama to the max here,' Helen carries on. 'Louisa arrived here after your fight, got super drunk and threw her phone into the sea. Then she threw up everywhere.'

At least that explains why Louisa didn't pick up any of Spook's calls. 'That's no way for a guest to behave,' I say, if for no other reason than to make sure she keeps talking.

'No,' laughs Helen, 'no indeed. When she woke up she decided she needed to go back home and sort out this shit about her course next year. Immediately. You know what she's like.'

'I do,' I say. In the darkness Helen's voice is like a string guiding me back. She is my Ariadne.

'Where are you, Grace?'

'Oh.' For two blissful minutes I'd forgotten about the hard rock I'm sitting on and the flat tyre and the disaster that is my life. A sigh works its way through me. 'It's kind of difficult to explain where I am. Literally.'

'Do you want us to come and fetch you?'

We? I cannot face Theresa. *Oh my god Grace, you swallowed a tray of pills? Your poor mum.* 'No, don't worry, it's fine.' I try and cover the misery I feel.

'You don't sound fine. Tell me what's going on.'

I start haltingly, but I am too tired to lie and soon the whole story is out. Helen waits for me to finish. 'So another average day, then.'

I laugh. Helen is my Ariadne and my angel in the sky. 'Exactly.'

'We're coming to get you. Brett will drive,' Helen continues.

'Brett? Didn't he take Louisa back to Cape Town?'

'Nope, Louisa's dad came to pick her up. They seem to have sorted everything out . . . Don't say anything to Louisa, but I think you had a point. She knows it too, that's why she got so upset. Anyway, Brett wouldn't leave while you were AWOL. How do we find you?'

Brett wouldn't leave without me? The words spread around my body like a warm current. 'I'm in a nature reserve, Gamkaskloof, in the Swartberg mountains; sitting under a sign that says *Die Hel*.'

Helen laughs. 'You couldn't make it up.'

'Helen's coming to get me,' I call to the torchlight walking towards me. I am surprised at the happiness in my voice. 'Phone works.' I hold it up when Spook emerges. He has brought with him a plastic crate holding pots and tins and a rolled-up foam mattress. Under his other arm is the gas canister.

'You not up for a night under the stars?' he replies, leaning forward and brushing a piece of hair out of my eyes. I look at him. This was my dream, I realise with a shock; we weren't lying on a raft, we were in the bush. 'See, that's the problem with your generation. No basic life skills.'

I feel sad looking back at him. Beneath the bush-coloured eyes and the grin that makes you want to be in on his joke, there is a part of Spook missing. He is not quite whole. *You're the one lacking the life skills, not me.* 'I think I've learnt enough life skills for one day,' I reply. 'We could give you a lift back if you want?'

'Nah,' replies Spook. 'Marvin is coming for me in the morning. But your friends are going to be a while. Might as well have some chow while we wait.'

'This stuff was in the boot of your other car. Do you carry it with you wherever you go?'

He straightens up. 'Of course.' He digs around in it and pulls out his navy jersey. 'You're going to need this,' he says, 'Trust me.'

I almost laugh out loud at how ludicrous that sounds, but I don't yet feel sure of which Spook is standing in front of me, so I pull it over my head.

'We need firewood before it's completely dark,' he carries on. After a moment I realise it is an instruction rather than an observation.

'How much darker can it get than this?' I call as I wander about the rocky ground, clutching the few dried-out twigs I can find without having to disturb whatever lies hidden in the bushes around us.

Behind me is a loud crack and Spook appears with two thick branches. 'Three a.m. dark,' he replies. He looks at my collection and tries to hide a smile. 'Haven't you been camping before?'

'Not like this,' I reply. Mum's idea of getting back to nature involves rustic cottages with no electricity. I shiver despite Spook's jumper – the mountain air has taken over.

'You need a drink.' He reaches into the crate and pulls out a bottle of Three Ships whiskey and an old thermos cup.

'No.'

'You're probably right.' He downs the whiskey in one glug and pours another.

I watch him unpack his bits and pieces and prepare the fire, breaking up and tearing off bits from the pile I collected with a nimbleness that reminds me of pick-up-sticks. He is quiet until it has a healthy glow.

'You thought they were coming after you,' I say as he fusses over the flames.

He sits back and looks at me. He picks up the thermos cup again and has a sip. 'There was a misalignment of expectations.'

'So they may still come after you?'

'At some stage. Maybe today; maybe tomorrow. Next year. It doesn't really matter.' How funny, I realise: he is the opposite of free.

'Why don't you report them?'

Spook shakes his head. 'It doesn't work like that.'

'It could. You could go away somewhere, it's not like you're leaving anything behind.'

'I could,' he says, nodding, 'I could.'

'Indonesia.'

'Yup.'

But I feel he's only agreeing with me to make me stop talking. He pulls a heavy silver penknife out of his pocket. It folds out to expose different sized blades and screwdriver heads. Who needs a gun when you have that?

The bush beetles and crickets magnify the quiet.

Spook unpacks a beat-up tin pot. It has a lid buckled to it. As he detaches it I realise it doubles as a plate. Inside the pot are a tin cup, a spoon and fork.

'That's clever.' My voice sounds unnaturally loud.

He looks up with his skew smile. 'Normally it's dinner for one.'

The words and the little-boy look tug at me but this time I could scream in frustration. He is made up of too many

191

contradictions. 'I don't understand how you can love the sea so much and be killing it at the same time.'

Spook sniffs but doesn't reply.

'Your lifestyle doesn't seem to make you particularly free,' I say. 'I can't make up my mind whether I should report you.'

Spook looks up sharply. 'For what?'

'Uh – poaching?'

'Jesus – that's fine thanks for saving your life.'

'You didn't save my life.'

He looks at me. 'I bloody did. You would have drowned, Grace.'

I glare down at my feet. The blue polish on my toes has turned dark purple in the firelight.

'So what did happen last night?'

Last night? I feel much older than the girl standing in front of the mirror. 'I needed to sleep.'

'Why?' asks Spook.

'Why?' I repeat with a hiss of anger, like one of the logs spitting in the fire. 'Because I was alone and I was scared that your gangster – sorry, *poaching* – friends would turn up again!'

'I don't think that was the only reason.'

'It was.' The Energade seems to have jump-started my stomach, and although I've been trying to ignore it, I need the loo. As I get up and walk past him, Spook glances up but says nothing. Night follows me as I walk away from the fire. I can't be more than a few metres off but I squat, holding onto a clump of nearby grass reeds to steady myself. I can feel darkness pressing into the earth and I am suddenly scared. I want to call to him, just to hear his voice, but something between Spook and me has shifted. All I am is my heartbeat thumping in my ears. All I see and feel and taste is darkness. Slowly the blood leaves my ears and my eyes start adjusting to the dark and shadows become bushes. Night grows louder and deeper as my heartbeat drops – rustling, a few crackling branches, the screek of crickets. Everything is hidden. Here even I am hidden.

So, what was that? asks a voice.

What? That was a beetle or something.

No, I'm talking about that.

The voice feels familiar. It could be internal or external because at the moment I can't tell the difference. The anger has left me vacant for the night to move in. But the voice tugs at me, I know it from before. It belongs to the other me behind the mirror in the bathroom. Oh God, not again. Now that she knows I know, she asks again, *what was that?*

Well that depends, are we talking about the bathroom and the pills, or the anger? The anger and I are old acquaintances. I have grown to need it. It has a bitter taste but it feeds me. Up until now. But it is the last thing I have to cling onto and I don't want to let go.

I shiver. 'I don't know,' is my truthful answer to the question. I don't know why I swallowed those pills. I don't really know who I am, what I'm supposed to be. But if I have learnt anything from meeting Spook, it's that you can't stop searching. And you can't run away.

Back at the fire, Spook is stirring something in his pot. 'Dinner is ready.'

'Dinner?'

'Spaghetti a la tin.' He hands me the plate with a mess of tinned pasta with chopped-up Vienna sausages.

I hold the plate away from my body. 'I can't eat that.' I say, trying to keep down the panic. How can a guy who is such a snob about his coffee eat tinned spaghetti?

'Rule number one of the bush: things you'd never eat taste amazing around a fire.' He hands me the fork. The strips of spaghetti are bloated, the tomato sauce a fusion of chemicals and artificial colouring. I don't dare look at the sausages.

'I'm waiting.'

Before today I'd have chucked it in the bushes but he's watching me from across the fire, holding the pot and spoon. Already the sauce is separating into its various indigestible ingredients. I lift a tiny forkful to my mouth. It is the most delicious thing I've ever tasted. I could eat bucket loads of it. I shrug and rest the plate on my knees.

On cue, the familiar argument in my head bursts back into life. One more forkful. Then I find I'm about to put another in my mouth and the panic starts and I put the fork back down. I sneak a glance at Spook who is already scraping the bottom of the pot. Imagine being able to eat a meal without thinking about every mouthful. I look back down at my plate and feel exhausted at the thought of all the meals that lie ahead, every day for the rest of my life. Spook puts the pot down and sighs in satisfaction. 'What happened with Louisa?'

'Ag.' I shrug. I eat another forkful of food, but it has lost all flavour. My stomach churns at the glutinous texture. I stare at the plate, blinking back the threatening tears. I get up and take the plate back to the pots. The mention of Louisa makes my heart contract. Her core is made of steel; the same strength that makes her brave also makes her utterly unforgiving when you cross her. I've seen it happen with other people. I never dreamt I'd ever feel it.

As if he can read my thoughts, Spook says, 'You're not a child any more. Grown-up relationships are different. Nothing is permanent, not even your parents. If you make it too difficult for someone to stay, they will leave. Trust me.'

'What makes you so very wise and still alone?'

Spook laughs. 'When you fuck up often enough you begin to see a pattern.' He falls into a silence. From the way his eyes flicker about, I suspect he does not enjoy looking at his pattern.

'Can I give you some more advice?'

'Don't accept tequila from strangers?'

He laughs. 'You have to let go, Grace.'

'Of what?'

'All that crap in your head. It's bullshit.'

'What am I supposed to do?'

'With what?'

'With this long, empty life ahead of me? Where am I supposed to go?' The words burst out.

Spook looks at me, his eyes crinkled up against the flickering flames. His two-day-old beard makes him look like a wild mountain man. He shrugs. 'You try one thing and then you try something else.'

'That's working really well for you,' I snap. 'Normal people have a plan. They have goals. Timescales.'

'Fuck normal people,' says Spook.

'Oh OK – so I'll just keep on keepin' on,' I say sarcastically. Spook considers this. 'Sounds about right.'

I watch him build up the fire. As he's rolling a joint, he glances up and catches me watching him. He gets up and comes to sit behind me. I lean back into him and let the cloying sticky smoke numb my exhausted brain.

'There are leopard in these hills,' he says when I think I'm already asleep.

'Bullshit,' I say loudly. I'd not even considered the possibility of leopard. They hunt at night. I shift closer to the fire.

'It's true.' He tops up his drink. 'But you're far too skinny. They won't bother with you.'

The approaching headlights wake me up. Spook is holding up his torch to hail them down. 'Are you sure you want to stay here?' I ask Spook.

'Hey, I'm good. Grace – before you go, I just want you to know.' I turn to him.

'Meeting you has been . . . important for me.'

'Important?'

'That's right.'

I smile at him. I have a feeling that although I'll probably never see Spook again, he'll be someone who lives in my head for a long time. Meeting him has been important.

I crawl into the back seat. It feels like crawling into a womb.

Spook leans in through the open window. 'Evening, folks,' he says to Brett and Helen. 'You guys were much quicker than I expected.'

'Nothing stands in the way of the mighty Ford Fiesta,' replies Brett.

Spook hands me my phone and wallet. 'Thanks,' I say. 'OK, then.'

He smiles. 'Fly on.'

When I turn back Spook is mock-saluting as Brett drives away.

Helen turns around and gives my hand a squeeze. 'We brought you a pillow and a duvet, my love.'

'Helen, I can't begin to describe how good it is to see you.'

WEDNESDAY

When I wake again, I'm lying in the middle of a double bed. Blue blinds block out the sunshine as best they can, but by the strength of the light shining around them, it must be afternoon. This is not Louisa and Brett's bed though – I suppose I must be at Helen's. Under the white fluffy duvet I am still wearing yesterday's clothes, including Spook's jersey. I sniff it. Wood fire and something else, more cloying. Sick, I realise.

When I venture into the rest of the house, it seems empty. There is a note stuck to the wall outside my room. *Gone to shops. Have a shower. See you soon, Hels.* Next to the words 'have a shower', Brett has scrawled, 'for all of our sakes'.

I smile and pull the note off the wall. In the bottom corner of the page Helen has written *PS PTO.* I turn the paper over. *One of those guys we met at that restaurant is a doctor. He's coming over later if there is anything you want to ask him.*

The house is similar to ours but more expensive. The passage is lined with blown-up photos of Helen and her family on various summer holidays. The shower in the bathroom could fit three people. My feet are encrusted with multiple layers of grime. My hair has returned to its original dirty brown colour. I stay under it for as long as I dare, washing myself over and over.

As I walk into the sitting room, wrapped in my towel, I feel a dread of the conversations that will have to happen. At least I still have a little while before they get back to think of something to say.

Helen's house has a similar view of the beach to ours, but theirs leads directly onto the beach. The living room opens onto a deep, shaded *stoep** with a red-and-white striped sofa and chairs and steps leading down to a sandy lawn. The wind today is nothing more than a teasing breeze. The sea is a dazzling blue. I feel the beach calling to me.

'Nice, huh,' says a voice behind me.

I spin around. Theresa sits up and stretches with the lazy grace of a cat in a coral bikini. She had been lying in the sun, hidden by one of the chairs. She puts on her sunglasses and takes a sip from a two-litre bottle of water.

'I thought everyone was out,' I say at last.

'I offered to stay behind. Brett has brought some of your clothes over. They're in that bag in the sitting room.'

'OK.' I turn, grateful to have a reason to escape.

'Grace,' she says.

I stop, already regretting what I feel might slip out any moment.

Theresa bundles her hair into a top-knot. 'I spoke to my mum this morning,' she begins.

* porch

200

You little cow, you self-satisfied bitch. The worst of it is that I'm standing in front of her in nothing but a towel.

'And I told her we'd spent yesterday and the day before on the beach. All of us,' she says slowly, looking at me.

'What?'

'She was worried about how you were getting on but I told her she was being silly.'

'Thank you, Theresa.'

'Now go and get dressed – with nothing on but that tiny towel, you're causing a sensation on the beach.'

Brett has brought me the hot pants Louisa bought and a T-shirt. As I'm leaving the room I glance back at Spook's jumper and pause. A part of me wants to put it back on, to hide inside it. *No.* Today I want to feel the sun on my skin and the salt-heavy sky.

Helen and Brett arrive back, laden with Woolies bags as I reemerge from the bedroom. 'It's the sleeping beauty,' says Brett.

'Ha ha,' I reply. I feel a knot of anxiety as I search for words. I want to explain myself to them, it is the least I can do. But I don't know how to start. 'Thank you,' is all I seem to manage. 'Thank you,' I repeat uselessly.

Helen scoops me up in a boob-heavy hug. 'Don't be silly. Louisa has decided that perhaps the sky is not about to fall on her head and has persuaded her long-suffering father to drive her back up this afternoon.' She gives me a last squeeze and then lets go.

As she turns to the shopping bags Brett catches my eye and winks.

'Now,' says Helen, 'are you hungry, my love?'

'Nah,' I reply automatically, then stop. *You have to let go of all that bullshit in your head.* 'Do you know what, Helen? I'm starving.'

NOW

It was weird going home to Mum. At the moment our relationship feels a bit awkward and fumbly. After being 'absolutely fine' around each other for eighteen years it is hard to be anything different.

I let her have her way. I agreed to do the three-month programme for emotionally disturbed adolescents. I decided to do a Spook and 'try something and if that doesn't work try something else'.

There are twenty of us from around Cape Town, all with some form of 'mad, bad, or sad'-ness. We have to attend all day, Monday to Friday. When you first arrive, you have to sign an agreement to not indulge in self-harm while you are here. A girl had to leave because she cut herself over the weekend. Everyone in the group was very angry; surely if she was cutting herself she needed help even more. But they like their rules around here.

Generally the others' lives are a lot more fucked up than mine. Some of their stories blow my mind. There's no one else here with an 'eating disorder' ('Let's call a spade a spade, Grace' were the psychologist's first words), which was both a disappointment and a relief. In fact, the therapists and social workers are not particularly interested in the not eating bit, apart from weighing me once a week and growling if I'm lighter. Here it's all about 'How does that make you feel?' and 'taking ownership of your anger'.

We spend the days doing art therapy and role-playing and other ridiculous activities. It's annoying how insightful a guided daydream can be. Sometimes the counsellors decide to give you a rough time and push you into dark places which is raw and rubbish, but overall it feels a bit like being in Rory's shitty office, except here they're never going to give up on you.

There is a boy here, two years older than me. He seems to focus on being as disruptive as possible, and drives the staff at the unit mad. I get stomach cramps from laughing at the things he says, but deep down I know he's a searcher. Like me.

Author's Note

Almost Grace grew out of a question that kept nagging me once I'd finished my first book, *Leopold Blue*. As with many books about teenage protagonists, *Leopold* has a strong 'coming of age' theme, and afterwards I found myself thinking about people and characters who *don't* want to grow up, and why. Then I thought, *And what would happen if you dumped two such characters together in a stressful situation?* – and about that time Spook and Grace arrived fully formed in my head.

I gave Grace many of the feelings I had when I was her age. As I neared the end of school I couldn't see a place for myself in the world and wanted to disappear. As I felt more out of control in the external world I turned inwards and found the perfect way to create order. We all have ways of coping in a stressful situation. The trouble starts when we allow these behaviours to cut us off from what it is we are finding difficult to cope with. As strange as it may sound, not eating is very addictive and all-consuming. It is a way of pushing back reality and change.

Spook, on the other hand, has chosen a Peter Pan life. On the surface he is free, and presents a very attractive alternative way of life. But beneath this carefree exterior Spook is stuck at a point in his life from which he is unable to grow and evolve as a person. It was important for Grace to understand that his freedom is illusionary.

The primary tension of the story was always about Grace and Spook's chance meeting and the sense of recognition they feel for each other. I do believe that some people come into our lives for a reason – and sometimes they are there simply to deliver a message. I attended a programme similar to the one Grace goes to at the end of the book, and one day a staff member said something to me that completely changed the way I saw myself. I didn't see him again after I left the centre, but because of those words he has probably been one of the most influential people in my life.

Grace doesn't leave Baboon Point 'fixed'; she leaves, instead, on the brink of a new phase of her life. What she understands at the end is that she's a 'searcher', someone who is compelled to find answers and meaning in her life. This characteristic will always propel her forward, sometimes into situations she finds uncomfortable. But knowing and accepting who she is means that Grace no longer needs to express her insecurities by punishing her body.

Thanks

I am incredibly lucky to have had the unfailing encouragement and brilliant editorial eye of Matilda Johnson and the Hot Key team. Thanks also to Emily Thomas, who, when I pitched my very sketchy idea for this book, simply replied, 'I trust you.' A terrifying response! And, as ever, to my agent, Claire Wilson.

So many people have contributed to this book. Special thanks to Mary McNicholas, Ninon Thomson, Atalanta Georgopolous, Sarah Morris Keating, Elspeth Morrison and Alison Nagle. Thank you Cath and Spark for sharing your house and the magic of the West Coast; and Josie van Helden for your ideas back at the very beginning. Also to Stephen Knight and Romesh Gunesekera.

Most importantly, to Johnny, Saffron, Bella and Viola. Your curiosity and delight with the world inspire stories every day.

Rosie Rowell

Rosie Rowell was born and grew up in Cape Town, South Africa. After completing a BA degree in English and Economics at the University of Cape Town, Rosie arrived in the UK on a short working holiday and never quite managed to leave. She now lives in the wilds of West Sussex with her husband and three children, but returns to South Africa as often as the bank balance will allow. She has recently completed an MA in Creative and Life Writing at Goldsmiths University of London. Her first novel, *Leopold Blue*, was published by Hot Key Books in 2014.

HOT
KEY
BOOKS

Thank you for choosing a Hot Key book.

If you want to know more about our authors
and what we publish, you can find us online.

You can start at our website

www.hotkeybooks.com

And you can also find us on:

We hope to see you soon!